BACK HOME

DAN L. WALKER

ALASKA NORTHWEST BOOKS®

To my brother Bill and all the universal soldiers,
who thought the fire couldn't burn them.

Edited by Michelle McCann

Cover: Anakin Fox / Shutterstock.com

Library of Congress Cataloging-in-Publication Data

Names: Walker, Dan L., 1953- author.
Title: Back home / Dan Walker.
Description: [Berkeley] : Alaska Northwest Books, [2021] | Audience: Ages 14 and up. | Audience: Grades 10-12. | Summary: In Southcentral Alaska, Sam Barger tries to help his Marine Corps brother Joe, just back from Vietnam, who struggles with alcoholism and post-traumatic stress disorder in the turmoil of the 1960s.
Identifiers: LCCN 2020055728 (print) | LCCN 2020055729 (ebook) | ISBN 9781513262697 (paperback) | ISBN 9781513262703 (hardback) | ISBN 9781513262710 (ebook)
Subjects: CYAC: Brothers--Fiction. | Post-traumatic stress disorder--Fiction. | Alcoholism--Fiction. | Vietnam War, 1961-1975--Fiction. | Family life--Alaska--Fiction. | Alaska--History--20th century--Fiction.
Classification: LCC PZ7.1.W348 Bac 2021 (print) | LCC PZ7.1.W348 (ebook) | DDC [Fic]--dc23
LC record available at https://lccn.loc.gov/2020055728
LC ebook record available at https://lccn.loc.gov/2020055729

Proudly distributed by Ingram Publisher Services.

LSI2021

Published by Alaska Northwest Books
an imprint of

WestMarginPress.com

WEST MARGIN PRESS
Publishing Director: Jennifer Newens
Marketing Manager: Angela Zbornik
Project Specialist: Micaela Clark
Editor: Olivia Ngai
Design & Production: Rachel Lopez Metzger

PROLOGUE

I like to remember Joe the way he was the day he left for Vietnam. He sat at the kitchen table doing his best Dad imitation, drinking coffee and smoking his Lucky Strikes in his Marine green and his California tan. I was cleaning up the last of the biscuits and gravy while Mom worried away at the kitchen that was already so clean you couldn't tell she'd cooked in it. Joe and I were silent, frozen in the moment except for the sound of my fork scraping the plate and his cigarette smoke curling up from his face as he stared out the window at the snow-covered yard and the dead pickup truck in the alley. It seemed kind of cool back then to think of Joe in a war, marching his way across the countryside with a bunch of buddies, fighting their way out of trouble like the guys on TV's *Combat*. Those soldiers always killed the Germans and got out of tight spots okay.

"Why don't you get that truck running so you'll have some wheels when you get your license?" Joe said. "All it needs is a starter and tune-up. The battery's probably shot too."

"Well, it's going to need a fender and a hood too," I said. "I don't think those dents will beat out." Joe grimaced when I said it, probably remembering the night he got drunk and skidded on the ice turning into the alley. The pickup hit a power pole, wrinkling the hood and left fender. He lied to Mom about it, but I doubt she believed him.

"Hell yeah, it's just sitting there. You should get after that. Besides, we'll need it when we go hunting. Dad would expect that, Sam. It's time you bagged your first moose."

Mom leaned on the counter. "You don't need to do that, Joe. Givin' Sam the truck like that. You're going to need it when you get back."

"Nope. When I get back, my combat pay is going to replace the Mustang. I got it all figured." He nodded his head, took the lastdrag off the cigarette, and snuffed it out in my empty breakfast plate.

I grimaced and looked sideways at Mom, hoping she hadn't seen his sacrilege. Then I remembered what was happening and knew she wouldn't say anything. A son going off to war could get away with smoking at the breakfast table and using a breakfast plate for an ashtray.

"Yeah, Joe," I said, thinking how I'd never had the chance he did, a chance to shoot a moose with Dad at my shoulder.

"Gotta go, Mom," Joe said. "Time to head to the airport. I'll warm up the car while you powder your nose."

Mom looked suddenly desperate and took off her apron. "Sam, finish up the last of these dishes before you catch the bus, sweetie, and tell your brother goodbye."

Joe winked and reached a hand across the table as he rose. We shook, and then he was gone, out the kitchen door. I followed him and called to his back, "Don't get shot over there."

ONE

Three months later I was parked at the back of a classroom, staring out the window at the rotting, dirty snow piled along the parking lot, wondering how much snow was left back home at the cabin on the bluff. I imagined the moss was starting to show through the snow under the trees and the first catkins popping on the willows. That's when Halverson sauntered in and ruined my daydreaming by rapping a knuckle on his desk. Halverson was a young teacher with bushy hair and a mustache. He wore bell-bottoms and a corduroy sports coat like some guy off a TV show, but his class was at least interesting. Today, he held up the *Anchorage Times* newspaper with a map of Vietnam on the front page. "Okay gang, I've got a really exciting assignment for you this week, something a little different. I think you're going to like it." We all rolled our eyes.

Six months ago, I didn't know much about Southeast Asia. Oh, I knew that it was somewhere close to China, and I knew Joe had joined the Marines so he could go there and fight for or against the Vietnamese—that part was confusing. I knew that just last year, my pal Billy's dad died there before anyone was talking about Vietnam.

And now here was Halverson bringing it up in social studies class.

"You know how when we read a book in literature class, we talk about characters and their motivation, what they want?" he said. "And how we talk about the setting and the plot? Well, that's how we are going to study Vietnam and the conflict we're involved in there."

I smacked David Nelson on the shoulder. "Sounds like just another research project to me," I said. "He's gonna make us do the work." David looked back at me and arched his eyebrows.

Half of the class seemed to already have an opinion. "My dad says we gotta bomb the crap out of them," someone yelled.

From across the room, "Yeah, they don't believe in God."

And then, "That's 'cause they're Communists."

"I don't think it's our business. Bombing doesn't solve anything."

Finally, Halverson raised both hands and said in his game show voice, "Enough, enough. Let's be cool here." Then he held up a coffee can. "I have all your names in here, and we're going to draw for partners using the fair and impartial hand of fate." He waved his right hand in the air for effect like he was on stage.

I noticed that David was waving his hand too. This wasn't David's style. It wasn't our style. The two of us hung in the back of every class, just two half-assed students hiding out and killing time until the bell rang. Now David's hand was in the air and his mouth was open. I reached out to stop him, but it was too late. "So, Halverson. What happened to free will and the rights of man to speak for himself?"

"Mr. Nelson," Halverson said to David, "as much as I believe in man's . . . or woman's rights, this is a whole different thing. I can't let you team up with Barger there and allow him to ride your coattails to another C- on a project. In fact . . ."

"But I don't even want Sam for a partner!"

Most of the class laughed, and the rest sighed in boredom. I sank lower in my seat trying to hide, but there I was right out in the open. "Sorry, David," said Halverson, "the die is cast."

"Huh?" David looked confused.

"You lose," I said. "Move on, dude. Maybe luck is on your side." I know David was angling for a partner willing to carry the water for him, and I couldn't really blame him.

Then Halverson went all *Dating Game* on us, drawing names from the can and calling them out in pairs. When he read, "Sam Barger and Karen Shafer," David wouldn't even look at me. Instead of Karen—probably the best student in the class—he was stuck with Roger Taggart, whose dad wanted to "bomb the crap out of them."

When that was all over, I sprawled at my desk playing it cool as Karen marched across the room toward me with her face in a knot. Some of the other girls in the class would have been fun to partner with. In fact, it was cool when you didn't have to think up a reason to talk to a girl, but Karen would be all business. She was a pretty girl, but too lean and intense for me.

"I bet you're feeling like a raffle winner about now," I said.

"That's exactly what I was *not* thinking." Karen stood at attention with her books held against her chest like she was afraid I might look through her blouse, which I would.

Halverson was writing a list of topics on the board under three headings: Characters, Plot, and Setting. "I'll give you three minutes to pick a topic," he said. "First come, first served."

Karen looked at the board then back at me like I was a wet dog about to sit on her lap and said, "Ho Chi Minh."

"Ho Chi what?" I asked. Karen pointed at the board and there it was, Ho Chi Minh, under the list of characters. "Whatever," I said, and I waved a peace sign across the room to David. He flipped me off.

"Well, raise your hand!" she said, pushing my shoulder. I made like she really pushed me and pretended to fall off my seat.

"Hey, Halverson," said I. "Ho Chi Minh!"

"Excellent! I'm expecting some righteous work from the two of you. I look forward to your oral presentations to the class on Friday! Be prepared and bring your best," Halverson said.

A chill ran through me and I slumped even lower in my seat. Halverson had done it to me this time. Yeah, Karen Shafer was a goody-goody, straight-A student and would work her butt off for this project, but she never talked in class, not one word. She aced all her tests and turned in perfect notebooks and papers that teachers waved in our faces, hoping we'd try to match her effort. This was all fine and good, but no way was she going to give this oral report. *Sam Barger,* I thought, *you're screwed.*

Karen sat with her hands in her lap like she was in church. I leaned in. "Did you hear that? *Oral report.*"

Karen's eyes got wide, and she gasped. "Does he mean an oral presentation in front of the whole class?"

"No, I bet we can do ours all alone in the bathroom! Just you and me."

"Quit joking. It's not funny at all."

"Beats writing a report." She didn't need to know this all made me nervous too.

"For you, maybe."

I left her sweating and headed for the table in the back of the room stacked with magazines. Of course she followed me and stood with her hands on her hips as I studied the magazine covers in search of inspiration. Who in the hell was Ho Chi Minh?

Karen nudged my elbow. "You better help with this report, Sam Barger! I'm not doing all the work!" With that she flounced off to the newspaper table, leaving me studying magazine covers with tired soldiers in green walking through the jungle. I started seeing Joe under a helmet like that, marching in a green line with his blue eyes tired and looking scared like the soldiers in the picture. When I turned the page and saw pictures of soldiers on stretchers with bloody bandages, I wimped out and closed the magazine.

That night I pulled down an encyclopedia and looked up Vietnam and Viet Cong. As long as I could remember, my trusty *Compton's Encyclopedia* had been a plane ticket to the rest of the world. When I was a kid back in the cabin on the bluff with no TV or friends around, I'd just hunker down with the encyclopedia, first looking at the pictures then, as I got older, reading the articles. That night I spent more than an hour with ol' *Compton's*. I read about Ho Chi Minh and the war with France and how the world powers tried to divide Vietnam into two countries that were supposed to vote on reuniting.

By the time I killed the light, I knew that Vietnam was a big mess, and I couldn't figure what my brother thought he was going to be able to do to fix it when the Marines sent him there. He'd be in Vietnam six months at least—longer, if the Marines could talk him into it—and he'd be up against soldiers that had been in the fight since World War II, which didn't seem like an even match, especially when the enemy was on their home court. The whole thing looked like a shit storm, and my brother was smack in the middle of it. Damn it, Joe!

TWO

Karen showed up for class Tuesday loaded for bear. She had a bunch of *Time-Life* books and a stack of magazines that she shoved at me even before the bell rang. "Start reading through these and see what you can find. We've only got three class periods."

"Yes, ma'am!" I saluted her and winked at David, but he wasn't paying attention anymore. "But I've got my own plan, sister." I headed for the bookshelf where I knew Halverson had the yearbook edition of my encyclopedia with updates that were only months old. That was the only problem with the encyclopedia; they went out of date fast. If he had the latest one-volume update though, it should have the most current information.

I spent the class period cruising the latest word on Ho Chi Minh, the so-called savior of Vietnam, and checked out the *US News and World Report* magazine. They didn't have as many flashy pictures of the war as *Time* and *Newsweek*, but the articles had lots of background about Ho Chi Minh. By the end of the class period, the leader of the North Vietnamese was becoming my new hero.

Karen and I only agreed on one thing: we needed to show the story of this guy's life and how he got to be the leader. "I think we have to show how Ho Chi Minh became subversive," Karen blurted. "Why he wants to spread communism. I mean, that's why we're there, right?"

"What have you been reading?" I said, "This is about independence and colonization. Vietnam was a French colony, and when they wanted freedom, Minh was the Man."

"But he's a Communist!" Karen crossed her arms and slumped back in her chair. "You are impossible."

"Hard, but not impossible," I said, grinning. "Don't listen to all that John Birch Society crap. If we had been with the Vietnamese after WWII instead of helping France, it would be completely different . . . I think, maybe." I could argue my point with Karen all day because she gets mad easily and loses track of what she's saying. I was still confused about the whole thing, but she didn't need to know that.

David came and hung with us toward the end of class when nobody wanted to keep working except Karen. The two of us supervised her drawing a timeline on a piece of poster board. "So, you guys going to do a Wanted poster for ol' Ho Chin Man?" David asked.

"That's better than Sam's idea," Karen said without looking up.

"Sam's an idiot," said David. "Just ignore him. You should have had me as a partner." He flashed his best flirty grin, and I socked him in the shoulder. "I can see it now. Just like on TV: Wanted, Dead or Alive, Ho Chin *Man*," he said.

I replied, "It's Ho Chi Minh. And actually, we are taking the hero angle. 'Ho Chi Minh, Father of his Country.'" To irritate Karen, I pretended to write it across the poster.

She brushed my arm away. "Don't you dare, Sam Barger!"

The bell saved me and I headed out with David, swimming through the currents of kids crowding the hallway. As we walked, David said, "Shit, Barger. You going to talk against the war? Is that what you're doing? Your mom's going to kill you, man. And if she doesn't, your brother will. You do remember where he is?"

"I know, my country, right or wrong. Don't I have a right to my own opinion?" I said. "And Joe, he just wants to be the hero. He doesn't know about what's really going on."

David shook his head. "And you do? It's your funeral, man." He cut through the crowd to reach his locker. "I'll see you in the lunchroom."

I was stowing my books in my locker when a hand stuffed a flyer in my face. I grabbed it and slammed the locker shut. The paper was hand-lettered and still smelled of mimeograph ink. *Join the Movement!* it read. *Silent protest against the war! Silent vigil Wednesday to honor the fallen in this senseless war! Rally in Cafeteria at lunch!*

Suddenly the hallway noise and the flood of bodies closed in, and I felt the hot sweat on my spine. I wadded the paper and threw it down.

"Barger, pick that up," a teacher growled across the hall. I glared at her and retrieved my litter and stomped off. I dropped it in the first trash can I came to.

That night I read more about the war in the newspaper. I read quotes from politicians saying things like, "We have to fight the Red Menace there or we'll be fighting them here on our own soil." Red Menace was their word for communism. Others said it didn't seem fair that the people in Vietnam had to choose between a dictator and communism. College students and other protesters were marching in the streets and staging sit-ins and walk-outs. More American soldiers had died yesterday, and it was hard not to think that Joe could be one of them. In my mind I saw only Joe, not a Marine, and he was fighting in the jungle alone against a faceless enemy.

By the time Friday came, Karen and I had waged a four-day truce and put together posters and a timeline for the big show. "You are going to do the talking, aren't you?" Karen asked. She was all decked out in a plaid skirt, knee socks, and a white blouse buttoned up like Fort Knox. I remembered to wear a clean turtleneck and bell-bottom jeans without gravy stains.

"Who, me? Captain Know-Nothing? You want a back-of-the-classroom loser like me to speak for you?" I tried to look surprised like I didn't see this coming, but I ended up grinning wolfishly.

"Okay, you did help a lot, but I made all the posters and the timeline. Please, Sam. Come on! You have to." Kids were pouring into the classroom, and we only had a couple of minutes to get ready. I had planned all along to do the talking, but I couldn't resist teasing Karen. The clock was ticking in her head and she shuffled from one foot to the other, chewing her lip. I leaned back in my desk and looked into the distance as if we had all day. I held out as long as I could. Her face was flushed and I thought she might wet her pants.

"Okay, give me some skin." I stuck out my hand, palm up.

"You mean you'll do it?"

"Yes, I'll do it. Actually, I was planning on it all along."

Instead of slapping my hand, she grabbed my fingertips and gave me a limp shake. "But you better not blow it! My grade is on the line!"

"Mine too. I need this to pass the class. Your A is safe with me, little lady. This is going to be great!"

Halverson was hanging out in the doorway with a cup of coffee in his hand. "All right, people! I could really dig it if we could get started!" The class scrambled to get ready. "I'm giving you five minutes, then this thing is happenin'!" I wanted to burn Halverson's modern slang dictionary.

David walked behind me and smacked me on the back of the head. "Yeah, get it on, Barger, get it on!"

"You cool?" I asked.

"Like a snowbank," he replied.

Karen looked pale like a snowbank, but colder. I thought I heard her muttering, "What have I done?" But maybe I just imagined it.

Raymond Jackson and Brent Baker were the first to present, and they stammered their way through a report on the US military in Vietnam. They went with the numbers: In 1960, about a thousand American soldiers were in Vietnam. In 1967, almost half a million. I never thought of my brother as a number before. Already over thirty thousand Americans had died fighting in Vietnam, and over two hundred thousand were wounded. Then Raymond, one of four Black students in the class, used the rest of their time reading statistics: the US population was ten percent Black, but they were almost thirteen percent of soldiers in Vietnam and fifteen percent of the casualties.

"Black brothers and poor white guys, that's who's fighting this war," he said. "You guys will be going too, if you don't get into college. As for me, I'm getting me one of them college deferments. Seriously working on my jump shot!"

Everybody laughed, and Halverson said, "Right on, brother!"

As Raymond walked back to his seat he muttered, "Ain't your brother, sucka." And everyone laughed again.

Halverson looked confused. He waved his arms and made a little speech explaining that deferments were legal ways to avoid being drafted in the military—like a bunch of high school boys didn't already know all about the draft and how it worked. "You can get a student deferment for going to college," he said. "A medical deferment if you are unhealthy, or a religious deferment if you are something like a Quaker and don't believe in violence for any purpose." A bunch of kids wanted to talk about that, but he cut off the debate and brought up the next speakers, two kids I didn't know.

Somehow this pair of geniuses thought they could tell fifty years of Vietnamese history in three minutes. According to them, the French tried to keep the place as a colony but got run out in 1954, and then Ho Chi Minh tried to unify the country under a Chinese form of communism. The United Nations and the USA came in to try and fix things, which just divided the country in two. I knew it wasn't that simple, so I was hot to go when we were called next.

"Mr. Barger, Miss Shafer, it's your turn!"

Oh boy, I thought, suddenly feeling a knot in my gut, and my big ideas vaporized, but I looked at Karen and shrugged my shoulders like I had it all figured out. As we walked up to the front of the room together, she glared at me with tight eyes and lips that said, *Don't blow this!* I hoped my pants weren't unzipped but was afraid to check. I cleared my throat. Suddenly, my hands could barely hold the notecards. Karen sat the posters in the chalk tray and leaned against the board, trying hard to be invisible. It was show time.

"Okay," I said. Suddenly, the room seemed long and wide, packed with strangers' faces, all staring, waiting, and judging. I couldn't recognize anyone. I was looking straight down the aisle between two rows of desks, and that aisle seemed to stretch away endlessly like a pathway to nowhere. For some crazy reason, I thought of that TV show, *The Prisoner*, and how all the escape routes the hero took ended up leading right back to where he started. There was no escape for me, so I took a deep breath.

"Okay. Okay." Another deep breath. I looked at my cards, but they were a blur, and I couldn't read them. I looked at Karen, then at Halverson. Suddenly, words came spilling out of my mouth: "What if I said that Ho Chi Minh was the George Washington of Vietnam?"

THREE

It felt good when I finally said it. Something broke loose and I just started talking. I forgot about the posters and the damn notecards. I forgot about Karen and Halverson and the kids in the room. I forgot about being nervous and just told the story of the man I'd been reading about for the last week. "You see," I said, "this guy was just trying to get independence for his country, like our man, George. Except Ho Chi Minh was a Communist." I ignored the skeptical looks on faces and guys in the back shaking their heads. Sam Barger was preaching the sermon he was born to preach.

I told how Ho Chi Minh and his followers had fought side by side with the Americans during World War II, and how after the war they tried to free their country from two big powers, France and China. "When he declared Vietnamese independence," I said, "Ho Chi Minh announced, 'All men are born equal: the Creator has given us inviolable rights, life, liberty, and happiness . . .' Sound familiar?"

Suddenly, Karen tapped me on the shoulder, and the class laughed. She pointed at the posters with her head. Her eyes were big and confused. The magic was broken. I stumbled over my words as I gestured to the posters with my messy magazine cutouts of Ho Chi Minh and the story of his life in Karen's tidy script. There were a map and a timeline with more photos cut from magazines. Finally, I got some facts out. "Here's all the stuff about his life. You know, where he was born and stuff."

Then Halverson called time. "All right! Sam and Karen, far out." We headed back to our seats.

"So, you believe that Ho Chi Minh is like George Washington?" Halverson asked from his post, leaning against the counter that ran along the window side of the room.

Karen flinched and stumbled, dropping her posters. "Sam said that, not me."

"Sam?"

I kept walking back to my desk, suddenly feeling tired, like I had been up in front of the class for the whole day. When I settled into my seat, I looked Halverson in the eye. "Yeah, he was the leader of the resistance against a colonial power. He wants to free his country, just like old GW."

Halverson smiled. "But Sam, isn't your brother in Vietnam right now? It sounds like you believe we are on the wrong side of this war."

I was too much of a Barger to back down, so I didn't even flinch. "He is, and we are." Then after a long pause, "So?" It sounded like a dare and I meant it that way. I crossed my arms and stretched my legs out under the desk in front of me.

The class was silent for a second then erupted into arguments. A sly smile flashed across Halverson's face then disappeared as he rapped on his desk for order. "Okay. Cool it, guys. Let's move along. Mr. Barger, that's heavy, real heavy."

I just shook my head as the class grew quieter, but I could hear kids talking about it for the rest of the period. They argued in hushed tones and ogled me like I was some kind of freak. Little squalls rolled through as different students opposed me during their presentations. Halverson just kept leaning against the counter at the side of the room. His arms were crossed, a tiny smile on his face. I studied him and decided this was all going according to his plan, like he *wanted* this turmoil. It felt good to be in front of the class speaking my mind, but now that my blood had cooled, I felt like maybe I should have kept my mouth shut.

After class, Karen grabbed my arm. "I should have known you would screw it up!" she said. "Ho Chi Minh! George Washington! Are you kidding? Where do you get this stuff? We'll never get a decent grade now, Mr. Antiwar Protester!"

I waved it off and walked away. I knew she wouldn't listen. I didn't know myself why I had blurted out like that instead of following Karen's tidy notes. No, I had to open my big Barger mouth and say what I really thought. Once I got started, it was like a rock rolling downhill—I couldn't stop until I hit bottom.

As I left class with my books under my arm, I saw the sneers, and no one walked near me. I moved out into the flow of people in the crowded hall. All I had said was that Ho Chi Minh was like George Washington, and that made all the sense in the world to me. Luckily I had the whole weekend for people to forget.

Unfortunately, I didn't forget, and on Monday I imagined I was walking around with a target on my back even though no one mentioned what I had said the week before. Then at lunch while I was eating alone, the smell of sandalwood incense came to me and with it was a girl's voice. "Hey, can I sit?"

I turned, and a small, freckled face under a mop of black hair smiled at me with eyes that caught the light.

"Uh, sure," was all I could find to say. I recognized the girl—she rode my bus. She was standing there in a white cotton blouse and a jean skirt with her hair falling around her shoulders.

"You're Sam Barger, right? They told me to look for a tall guy with a big nose."

I blushed and forced a smile. "Yup, that's me." I suddenly felt like my nose was the size of my foot.

"Can I sit here and pester you bit?" Her eyes twinkled, and I remembered being too shy to talk to her on the bus.

"Yeah, sure."

She plopped her sack lunch down on the table and put her hand on my shoulder as she swung a leg over the long bench seat.

"It's not as big as it looks," I said.

"What?"

"My nose. It's not as big as it looks. It's just my face is so small."

She laughed, and she was embarrassed this time. "Oh crap, that was pretty tacky, wasn't it?" She put her hand on my shoulder again, and I liked that. "It's fine, really . . . your nose, I mean."

"Don't worry about it. I figure I'll grow into it. I'm already six foot though, so I guess I'm going to be ten feet tall."

Then we laughed together. "I can't stand eating alone," she said, "and I don't have many friends who eat lunch in the cafeteria, so I guess you're stuck with me." She unpacked peanut butter and jelly on homemade whole-wheat bread, a carrot, and two oatmeal cookies. I was nearly finished with my meatloaf, so I slowed down to pace my eating with hers. She took a bite, chewed a bit, and then leaned over and took a swallow from my milk carton.

"I heard about your thing in Halverson's class last week. I have him first period. He told us what you said and about Ho Chi Minh and George Washington. All that."

"He did?" I wasn't sure whether to be proud and worried.

"Oh yeah. You know Halverson, Mr. I'd-be-cool-if-I-could. He used it to start a discussion about the war, pro and con. You know how he is."

That made me laugh. "Anyway," she continued, "he got us in a big debate about it and a lot of kids are talking about it now. That's why I'm here."

"So it's not about my nose at all?"

She punched my shoulder. "Quit it. I'm trying to be serious here." But she laughed anyway. I liked that laugh. I liked the attention from this girl I'd only noticed in passing before. "We're organizing a protest. And I thought you might want to come."

I couldn't resist. "Against my nose? That's not very nice."

"Oh, you are such a brat!" She punched my shoulder like a guy might, and I was starting to enjoy her close to me.

"No really, what protest? Like a sit-in?"

She smiled like I was some lame, know-nothing dipshit. "Oh, so you really don't know. You didn't get the flyer?"

"Oh, that." I gritted my teeth and finished my mashed potatoes and the last bite of meatloaf. I remembered someone handing me a flyer on Friday that I'd thrown away. I hadn't really read it. While I chewed, we had what Mom calls a pregnant pause, when not saying anything was noisier than talking.

The girl broke the silence and started to leave. "Really? 'Cause I could just go now. Should I go? I should, huh?"

"No. It's cool. Hang out."

She relaxed a little and finished her sandwich. "I'm going to just say this one thing, you know . . . anyway. I just think . . . I mean, I thought since you made the big speech in Halverson's class . . . I thought this might be your thing. You know. Join the cause for peace. You made a big statement for all of us when you spoke out in class."

"Yeah. Well, you see . . ." I said. She handed me a cookie—chewy oatmeal with raisin, my favorite. "It's not a big thing . . . what I said. It was just a stupid class presentation." Then I saw that her eyes were brown with long lashes, and she had freckles sprinkled like glitter across her cheekbones, and I surrendered. "Sure. I'm in," I said. *I'm in all right*, I thought. I'm so far in I'm almost drowning.

"Great! Do you like the cookies? I made 'em."

"Yeah, I love chewy oatmeal," I said with a full mouth.

She smiled. "I'll remember that." At that point she could ask me to rob a bank, and I would have asked which branch. But she didn't stop. "Is it true that your brother is over there? In Vietnam?"

I swallowed the last of the cookie and wished there was more. "Yup. But that doesn't matter. He just wants to be a Marine and prove himself," I said. "I don't get it." I really meant I didn't want to talk about it.

"It must be tough though."

"You might say that." She looked at me with her brow wrinkled and nodded her head, but she didn't ask anymore about it.

"Here's the deal," she said, turning businesslike again. "As you probably know, we aren't allowed to protest on school grounds, so Wednesday we are walking into the cafeteria and sitting at a table silently for the whole lunch period, a silent fast for peace. What do you think? Will you *not* eat lunch with me on Wednesday?"

Crap! Who could refuse?

I spent the evening humming Van Morrison's "Brown Eyed Girl" and thinking about those freckles and the taste of her cookies, and the way she said I spoke for all the kids against the war. I couldn't think about that though without Joe elbowing his way into my mind.

I kept remembering when Joe had come home from basic training, lean and tan in a green uniform that he wore like a store mannequin. Every button glimmered like gold, and his shoes reflected light like the fender of a new car. His hair was short the way Dad used to cut it when we were kids so that even the back of his head was tan, and his neck seemed as big as his head. When Joe walked up the driveway from the taxicab he had moved like Dad, rolling from side to side as if he walked the deck of a ship. Marine basic training had changed a gawky boy into He-Man in five months.

I remembered Mom had rushed out to wrap herself around him while I'd stood in the doorway, feeling suddenly small and sloppy in my shaggy hair, jeans, and T-shirt. "My lord, you are the spittin' image of your father, I swear," she'd said when she got her breath and pushed Joe back to look at him.

"Aw, Ma." He had been restless, his eyes looking past her. "Who's this long-hair hanging around my doorway?" he'd asked, only half-friendly.

"Hey, Joe." I'd pushed my hair back and over my ears. "How's it going?" I was nearly as tall as him then, but Joe was broader and more muscular.

"Well, it was going pretty good until I saw my little brother turned into a hippie while I was gone."

"It's just hair."

"Just hair? Just hair like a draft dodger or war protester. That's how it looks to me." He'd set his duffel on a kitchen chair and lit a cigarette.

"Now, boys. Don't start off this way." The two of us had backed away from each other with our chests out while Mom had pushed past us into the kitchen to turn the pork chops working in the cast iron skillet. Joe'd picked up the duffel and marched stiffly into the living room then pushed the bag into my stomach.

"Stow this," he'd said.

It started hard that way and never got soft. I looked at Joe, and I was full of questions I couldn't ask. I wanted Joe to talk about boot camp and why he volunteered in the first place, but that conversation would have to wait. I wondered if Joe remembered about going hunting like he promised. It was one of the last things he had said before leaving: "When I get back, we're going moose hunting, just you and me."

After Joe shipped out to Vietnam, Mom kept a picture of him in his dress uniform on top of the TV in front of the rabbit ears, so he stared at us while we watched *Star Trek* and *Bonanza*. I would find Mom standing at the sink looking out the kitchen window with her hands clenched around a towel so tight that her knuckles turned white. She was thinking about Joe and the grim possibilities that surrounded him. I felt the same helplessness I did when Dad died, and instead of hugging her or telling her something comforting, I avoided her because I didn't think comfort was possible. The photos in magazines and on the nightly news made the war look hot and bloody and real every day. I wondered how anyone could feel good about us being a part of it.

It was one thing to be against the war and keep it to yourself; it was a whole different thing to say it to a class of thirty kids. Now I was about to walk into a cafeteria full of people and announce that Sam Barger was against the war his own brother was fighting in. I made a statement all right, but I had a feeling I was going to pay for it.

FOUR

Two days later I walked into the noisy, crowded cafeteria to not eat lunch with thirty people I hardly knew. The silent peace protesters were sitting at a table under a painting of a giant red-and-blue thunderbird, our school mascot. Taped to the ends of the table were signs reading, *Fasting for Peace—Join us!* I felt the eyes of kids at other tables watching as I bypassed the food line and crossed the room to join the protest.

It was easy to spot the right table since most of the guys wore their hair as long as the school rules would allow and had peace symbols on chains around their necks. Girls with loose hair and beads wore billowy bright skirts like the hippie girls on TV. These were the kids we didn't see in the cafeteria much because they spent their lunchtime smoking and eating spiked brownies out in the student parking lot. None of the popular kids were there and none of the athletes. Just the hippies and few of us who didn't have a group to hang with. You could spot us pretty easily. Boys with our buttoned shirts and Levi's, and girls in corduroy jumpers or knee-length wool skirts, their hair curled and held in place with hairspray.

The whole table was silent. I said hi to the few kids I knew and looked around for the brown-eyed girl, hoping we could sit together. She stood up so I could see her and pointed to an open spot at her end of the table. She was dressed in bell-bottom jeans with flowers embroidered along the seams, and an army fatigue jacket that was too big for her. A guy in a navy pea coat that looked like he wore it all the time, even to bed, sat on the other side of her and gave me the are-you-my competition stare. I grinned like I knew what I was doing and grabbed an open spot on the bench beside her. She gave me a friendly shoulder bump.

Other students were filling the long cafeteria tables with sack lunches or trays from the lunch line steaming with turkey and gravy. *It's going to be a long time 'til dinner,* I thought. My second thought was how much I hated being so conspicuous. Kids stared as they walked by and chuckled with their friends after they sat down. Of course a few came and joked around trying to get us to talk, to break the silence. And a few called us names as they passed us.

After about fifteen minutes of smelling turkey and fresh-baked rolls, my stomach growled and gave everyone at my table a good whispered laugh. Then a dinner roll sailed across the room and smacked the table with a wet spatter of soggy dough. That was followed by an empty milk carton. I turned and saw three seniors standing across the room, laughing and congratulating each other. The tallest one launched a wad of wet napkins that hit the brown-eyed girl in the back. I was halfway out of my chair when she grabbed my arm and pulled me down. I clenched my teeth and glared across the room.

I had to be satisfied with flipping them the bird, which got one of them starting across the room toward us, but just then Vice Principal Parker appeared in the middle of the cafeteria as if out of nowhere. "All right, people! Knock it off."

Parker was small man with a beer belly who walked with a swagger like he was looking for a fight. Halverson stood behind him chewing his lip. Another teacher rushed in and put a hand on the vice principal's shoulder and showed him a clipboard.

Parker nodded and said, "Everybody stay put! Nobody, and I mean nobody, move a muscle!" His face was red and his neck bulged around his collar like his tie was choking him. The whole cafeteria was suddenly as silent as our protest table. He stabbed a finger at clipboard. "I want the name of every kid at this table." The teacher looked us over and put his pen and clipboard to work.

The vice principal walked directly to our table and shook his finger at the brown-eyed girl. "Young lady, I told you people that there were to be no protests or demonstrations of any kind in this building or on school grounds. Did I not?"

Suddenly inspired, I raised the two-fingered peace sign above my head, and then everyone at the table did the same. I stared Parker square in the eye when I did it, and the girl beamed at me like I had done the one perfect thing for that moment.

Her face was flushed, but she stood up and stuck her chin out. I stood with her—like I could do anything. "It's not a demonstration," she said. "We're just sitting together not eating. What's wrong with that?"

"And this?" He grabbed the hand-lettered sign. "Did this just happen to be here on your table?" He crumpled it in his hand.

I couldn't stop myself from speaking up. "It's a free country. Even for us. We got rights." My hands were on the table, and I leaned toward him.

Parker turned a hard face to me. "Can it, Barger. No one's impressed." I threw up my hands in frustration and turned to Halverson, hoping he'd be there for us, but he just shook his head and tugged at his tie. He shifted nervously and wouldn't make eye contact.

We got a tiring lecture from Parker, and then he said, "You people will remain here for the rest of the school day. I'll be contacting your parents, and you can expect you won't be in school tomorrow or the rest of the week for that matter."

That got a general chuckle out of half of us, and everyone else looked pale and worried. I was too pissed to care about missing a couple of days of school. "And how about those jerks throwing food at us?" I insisted. "What about them?"

Parker was unmoved. "I told you to shut up, Barger. It's over. Your little troupe here has interfered with the learning environment of the school. I won't have it."

I sat next to Brown Eyes who got me into this in the first place, and we looked at each other and wrinkled our brows, then laughed. "Interfered with the learning environment of the school—whatever that means," I said.

She shook her head and leaned in. "I think it means we pissed him off."

"I guess it means I get to spend the rest of the day with you," I said. "We should do this more often."

"You know," she said, ignoring my attempts to flirt, "in some places, they are calling out the National Guard with guns. Can you believe they are tear-gassing students for protesting? So much for land of the free. Imagine what they are doing to the people in Vietnam." That brought up images of Joe in full combat gear carrying an M-14 through a village of scared Vietnamese. It's hard to think of my brother that way. Hard as hell.

I scooted closer because we weren't supposed to be talking. "I saw on the news where lots of those National Guard soldiers only joined the Guard so they wouldn't have to go to Vietnam. Instead, they're playing Gestapo here at home." I wanted to sound like I knew was I was talking about, but I was really winging it all afternoon. I had come to the cafeteria just to impress this girl, but now this was starting to feel important. It might be worth it, after all, to stand up for what I believed, even if Mom and Joe got pissed at me. Either way, I got spend the afternoon with the freckle-faced girl with bedroom eyes. Every cloud has a silver lining.

After school, getting out of the building was like running the gauntlet. "Hey, Barger! I hear you organized a peace march in Halverson's class," said Josh Martin, a kid skinny enough to hide behind a signpost. His Beatle boots and pegged pants made him look like a scarecrow.

"Yeah right, that's me," I said, "puttin' it to the man." I didn't stop to chat.

"Hey, Sam!" Mary Belnap yelled. "Been nice knowing ya! Bye bye." She was at her locker when I walked past. Her eyes were big and excited like the police were on the way and I needed to run.

"What?" I asked.

"Well? Didn't you get suspended or something? That's what I heard," she said.

"I'm here, ain't I?" This was getting absurd.

Another kid stuck his pimply nose in. "Comrade Barger, bet your brother kicks your ass when he comes home on leave."

I had to push off people's shoulders to pass down through the crowd, bouncing like a pinball toward the doors and freedom. Then I heard a voice from behind me. "Hey Barger, a bunch of guys from Fort Rich is callin' you out."

That's all I needed, guys who lived on the Army base coming after me. I banged through the double doors and grabbed a lungful of freedom. My stomach had a knot the size of a basketball, and I was feeling woozy.

I almost made it to the bus before three guys in letter jackets plowed through the crowd of kids lined up to board. They were making a beeline for me, and I knew it. And I didn't need a suspension for fighting tacked on the one I had already.

"Hey Barger, you punk!"

I was three steps from the bus door and knew I wouldn't make it in. No way I could reach the safety of the bus before this senior letter-jacket asshole arrived to punch my lights out. I knew that was his plan because Jacob Phelps was always looking to kick someone's ass, and he never came alone when he did. This time he had two sidekicks, I guess just in case I turned out to be some John Wayne, nose-busting guy who he couldn't handle. It didn't look like that would be a problem. Phelps was nineteen going on thirty, and had blacked more eyes than anyone else on this side of town. "Yeah, Barger, I'm talking to you," he said.

From the corner of my eye, I could see the bus driver sitting sideways in his seat, eyes fixed on Phelps. Phelps must've seen it too because he didn't stop. He walked past me on the sidewalk, letting his shoulder slam me into the side of the bus. Then one of his buddies elbowed me as he passed, muttering, "Chickenshit." He was hoping I would take a swing, hoping I would give him one chance to defend himself in front of this crowd, hoping I'd be his willing victim.

I raised my hands in surrender, and said, "Whoa!" like you do when you're crossing a street and a car comes too close. Just "Whoa!" That's all I said, and David Nelson was kind enough to laugh. Then I laughed too when it was too late for those assholes to hear, too late for them to come back and kick both our asses, and they probably would even with the bus driver right there.

I think everyone on that damn bus had something to say. It was like running a gauntlet of words.

"Hey Barger, I thought you were a goner."

"Whoa, somebody's in for an ass whuppin'."

"What's going down, man?"

"You the dude who did the peace protest in the cafeteria?"

There was noise from every direction, and then there she was, the brown-eyed girl sitting in the third row back from the driver. "Well, at least someone is standing up against the Establishment!" she said loud enough for everyone to hear. I saw the sunlight on her face before David pushed me down the aisle toward an open seat.

"There's the girl for you," said David, giving her the nod. "You two could start the Make Love, Not War Club."

I punched him. "Yeah, I know. She's all right."

Then I looked up and she was standing beside me.

"Hey," she said. "Wanna fight?" She put up her fists like a boxer.

"I don't know. You look pretty tough."

She tucked her hair behind her ear and sat down in the seat in front of us. She turned and said, "Thanks for coming today."

"Was nothing," I lied. David was silent and looking lost like he'd started watching a movie halfway through.

She shook her head. "No, it was something." She was kneeling on the seat facing back at me, and I felt suddenly important like all this attention might not be all bad.

"I know it is something, but it's not like LBJ's going to end the war because we want him to."

The bus driver looked in the rearview and asked, "Hey young man, you want me to wait while you go take care of those fellows in the letter jackets?"

"I don't have time for punks like that," I said. "And I'd hate to make everybody wait."

He laughed. "You sure? I don't mind." I laughed too. The brown-eyed girl just pointed her freckles at me, shook her head, and frowned.

"I'll hold your coat!" volunteered David.

The girl turned her back to us.

"We could have taken those guys. It was only three against two," I joked. We laughed again. I was able to act all cool and clever, but my guts were churning and I felt my connection with the girl slipping away. I kept looking at the mound of black hair in front of me, and I smelled a sweet, pungent odor coming from her like incense but sweeter. I wanted to talk to her more, but I couldn't shake the jitters, so I just sat. Part of me wanted to run, but part of me was also feeling strangely elated, and not just because I met a girl either.

I wasn't home yet though, and Mom was bound to have a lot to say about me getting suspended and even more about why I got suspended. As Dad used to say, dinner was going to be hot tongue and cold shoulder.

FIVE

"You kids all think you're so damn smart," Mom said, stopping her knitting to shake a foot-long needle at me. "You think the rest of us are all a bunch of fools who are out to make your lives miserable." After the school called, she hadn't said a word to me. But now she was in her easy chair watching Walter Cronkite report the news on the TV, and, of course, they showed footage of kids protesting the draft and burning draft cards.

"Come on, Mom!" I said. "Look, even Walter Cronkite says the war is wrong, and he was there. He's not some smartass kid." I thought I had her then. Walter Cronkite was a crusty old anchorman who everyone respected, at least until he spoke out against the war.

"Watch your mouth, Samuel. And let me tell you something, mister. Your father and a lot of other men put their lives on hold to fight and die so that little smart alecks like you could have the right to march around and have your little protests. So men like that can say what they please." She gestured at Cronkite with her knitting needle. "I mean, look at those silly young men with their long hair and sandals, those girls with no bras. Lord have mercy."

"Times are changing, Mom."

"That may be, but I never want to hear again that you've been causing trouble at school with your little political protests. What's gotten into you?"

"Mom, do you really think Joe should be over in Vietnam putting his life on the line? For what? Why are we even over there?" I didn't have much ammunition, but I wasn't in the mood to back down or shut up.

She just shook her head turned back to her knitting. "Don't talk to me. I have to count stitches."

The next news story was more footage of protest marches and sit-ins being staged around the country. Lines of people, mostly young folks, were marching arm in arm down big-city avenues. Then there was another scene of college students fighting with the police. Part of me felt a bit of pride in being a part of what was on the news.

Mom started in again. "And as for your so-called protest in the cafeteria, you can spend your days off from school cleaning this house from top to bottom, and don't even think about going anywhere. Now, look at that. All those people making fools of themselves. It's just silly."

"But Mom, they're there because they think the war is wrong. Don't you get it?"

"Sam Barger, there is no Christian in the world who is happy about killing people, but sometimes we have to do unpleasant things, and this is one of them. Someone has to step up and draw the line against that godless communism." The news went to commercial, and the next story was about movie stars Richard Burton and Elizabeth Taylor's current marriage woes.

That didn't stop me. "Oh come on! Who wouldn't choose communism over some dictator? And it's not like we are doing so much better there. Like how they treat Black people in the South. Why do think they are marching?" I leaned forward in my chair, frustrated with Mom just sitting in her chair knitting like we were talking about the weather. She wasn't all fired up like I was, and that was irritating.

"Sam. When you're older, you will understand. Do you really think that a bunch of young kids like you knows better than President Johnson and all his advisors? And he is our president whether you like it or not. Now go put on the kettle so I can have some tea."

"Walter Cronkite, Mom, Walter Cronkite." I shook my head as I headed for the kitchen, wanting to yell at her and kick the wall, but instead I got her tea.

"It's wrong, you know," I said as I served her with a fine china cup and saucer. "It's all wrong no matter how old you are." And with that, I figured I had the last word and retreated to my room, hoping that by Monday morning I could go back to being the invisible guy in the back of the classroom.

By Saturday, my ass was raw from Mom chewing on it, and I had spent two days as Sam the housemaid, scrubbing floors and vacuuming and washing down the kitchen. I cleaned the whole damn house and was glad we lived in our little bungalow and not some big split level.

With the laundry put away and the kitchen ready to be on a magazine cover, I wrapped a baloney sandwich in a paper towel and went out to the GMC parked in the alley against the chicken wire and picket fence. Usually, my daydreaming could transport me to anywhere I wanted to go. Not today though. Today, the tinny sounds from my portable transistor radio brought me Buffy Sainte Marie's "Universal Soldier." For the first time, I actually listened to the words. She sang about soldiers throughout history being the basic weapon of war. Her voice reminded me of the brown-eyed girl trying to put an end to war, and the words made me think of Joe.

My mind was a ping-pong ball bouncing from the girl I just met to the war, to Joe, and back again. What would I do if my draft number came up when I was eighteen? Was I ready to be a universal soldier? Sure, I could brag that I would run to Canada like some guys who were dodging the draft, but could I do that to Mom and Joe? Where did a guy get advice for a decision like that? The ping-pong ball kept bouncing, and I was back in the truck I had promised to get running.

When Joe gave me the keys to the '57, it seemed like the answer to a prayer, but now the truck was still sitting in the alley, just a place to hide like the tree fort back home on the bluff. I had lots of plans for the truck, but they all cost money. With nothing but the odd lawn work and babysitting jobs, money was in short supply.

I used the paper towel from my sandwich to wipe off the dashboard and the steering wheel. The truck had collected a lot of dust since Joe left, and he liked his cars spotlessly clean. Even in the sloppy weeks of spring breakup, Joe's ride was always washed and waxed. Even when it was washed and waxed, the GMC pickup wasn't much to look at. The fenders were starting to rust and the inside of the bed didn't have much paint left. The green body paint had grown dull, and cracks spread like a spiderweb across the windshield. Now the truck was so dusty it looked abandoned, but I felt right at home sitting in it. If I could start it up and drive away, the Seward Highway was only a few blocks away. In four hours, I could be back at the bluff where it all began, back where I wanted to be.

Back before we left the beach, back before we left the cabin on the bluff, back before a lot of things, they called me the family moose spotter 'cause I spotted that first moose Dad ever shot. I carried that with me for a long time, a sign of the great hunter I'd be someday.

I was only five then, and we had just gotten the roof on the cabin and moved in. Dad and I had been coming up from the beach in the

Jeep with a load of coal. The Jeep was an old Army surplus rig with no top and a broken windshield, so we were bundled deep in our coats against the cold wind coming off the Cook Inlet. The beach road followed a creek up through the bluff and wound through the woods for a hundred yards to the highway. From there it was only a quarter of a mile to the road that led back to where our cabin perched on the bluff. I remembered the clearing was rough and ugly then, like an open wound in the forest where the skin of moss and brush had been scraped off leaving furrows of dirt and roots.

The Jeep had just crawled over the edge of the bluff to the flat part of the road when I'd spotted the dark rump of a moose sticking out from behind a birch blowdown. "Moose, Daddy! Right there!" Dad had hit the brakes, standing up as he did and grabbing the windshield. Just then, the moose had stepped out and showed a wide set of antlers.

"Damn," Dad had whispered, "I forgot the aught-six!"

"Shhh, Daddy! Don't spook him. Let's go get your gun."

Dad had laughed, shifted the Jeep into first, and gently pressed the gas pedal. The two of us had grinned and nodded at each other as he'd shifted up and accelerated slowly toward the highway. We had us a moose less than a mile from the house and no rifle. If we could sneak by without spooking him, there was a chance, just a chance, that we could get to the house and back with the aught-six before the animal moved on out of sight.

Dad's aught-six was a World War II rifle with a full wooden stock. It always rested on two pegs just inside the cabin door, loaded and waiting. In ten minutes, we had gotten back with the rifle, and Dad put a 170-grain slug right behind the mule-sized ear. The Bargers' first moose was down, and I was the one who had spotted it.

"We made meat today!" Dad had whooped. "You're a regular Hawkeye, Sammy, spotting that old moose that way." I knew right then I was meant for the forest, for the hunt, for making meat.

It seemed from that day on the woods became my world. I studied animal tracks, calls, and even droppings until I could recognize any track I found in the snow. I could separate the coyote's call from the howl of the neighbor's sled dogs and the voice of the wolf. When I wasn't at the beach site and thinking about fishing, I was in the woods or studying animal books.

Sometimes Joe and I would hike to the edge of a small pond behind the house. Loons lived there, and he showed me how to recognize their call and the call of the trumpeter swan. I learned to spot the whooping cranes that appeared like loose strings of beads thousands of feet overhead.

All that was ten years ago, and now things seemed so insanely different. Dad was gone, Joe was in the Marines, and our sister, Mary, had a husband and a kid. It's not like I became someone else, but more like I was separated from that person I used to be. I was almost split in two, Sam Now and Sam Then—two different people separated by a death and war and events that had run over me like a porcupine on the highway.

SIX

David Nelson likes to show up at dinnertime, and this Saturday was no exception. Mom faked surprise. We sat around the small table in the kitchen with a window that looked into the backyard where the melting snow was exposing the dead grass. The kitchen was bright and clean the way she liked it, and she was looking fancy, still dressed in heels and nylons from work. I watched her light up when David took Joe's place at the table and added a voice to our dinnertime conversation.

David's mom worked nights, and he got tired of hanging around their trailer house by himself. Not that our house was any nicer, but there were people in it. We lived in a two-bedroom bungalow in a neighborhood full of others like it. Me and Joe shared a room when he was home, and Mom used to share her room with Mary until my sister got married and moved to Fairbanks. I had looked up the word "bungalow" once when I read it in a story, so when Mom bought this house, I realized it was a bungalow, which sounds more stylish than saying we're living in a little house. When I first told David it was a bungalow, he had laughed. "Like my house is a mobile home, not a trailer," he had said. We were fast friends after that.

"David, I'm glad you're here to help us clean up all this slumgullion," Mom told him. "I don't know who I thought I was cooking for. I made enough to feed an army—or the two of you." She was stirring her concoction in an electric skillet full to the brim with the macaroni, hamburger, and tomato mixture that I had been eating once a week all my life. "Truth be known," she said, "I don't know how to make any less."

David smiled. "Thank you, Mrs. Barger. I'm glad to help with that."

I jumped on that. "Good, you can do the dishes."

"You can both do the dishes and mop the kitchen floor while you're at it," Mom said. "I've got a date with an Ellery Queen mystery."

"I thought you had a date with us," flirted David.

"You behave yourself," she said. We all laughed, and for a brief moment the whole world seemed pretty darn okay.

David and I cleaned the kitchen and went out to sit in the truck and listen to music. "You seriously need a stereo in this rig," David said. "And wouldn't it be sweet with a four on the floor and some muscle under the hood."

"How about I get it running first. Then I'll work on some tuck and roll leather upholstery and chrome rims," I laughed.

"Yeah, that's a good idea too." David pulled two cans of beer out of his coat pocket. "But for now we got cheap beer and rock 'n' roll on Barger's little radio."

"All right! You brought dessert," I said. "I could sure use one. Where'd you get these? You got a fake ID now?"

David popped a beer open and took a sip. "Shit, there's a place by my house you don't need ID. If you got cash, they sell to you. Piece of cake."

We sat sipping our beer, listening to the Top Forty countdown. Then David asked about the protest. "So what's up with you and that antiwar stuff? I didn't know that was your thing. Or was it the girl on the bus?"

A cool wind was blowing down the alley, so I rolled up a window I had opened when David lit his cigarette. Spring's longer daylight and melting snow promised summer was coming, but the air was still wintry feeling. "Well, a little of both," I said. "She came and sat with me at lunch and talked me into it, so what the heck."

"She is cute, in a hippie chick sorta way." David swigged his beer and laughed. "Maybe she's into free love. You might get lucky there, buddy, and pop your cherry." He nudged me with an elbow.

I suddenly wished it was her sitting with me in the pickup cab instead of David. "I'm not just in it for a piece of ass, man," I said. "But I wouldn't turn it down."

"Give it time, my man. I saw how she looked at you with those bedroom eyes. But three days' suspension for little protest? That's harsh, man,"

"Hey, it wasn't a little protest! At least we're doing something." I turned down the radio so I could hear David better than the DJ running down the hit singles list.

"That's not what I meant. It's just that you guys weren't really bothering anybody. Shit, if things are going to change, it's up to us. Hell, in another couple years it'll be you and me marching off to war because some politician's got a hard-on for some little country in Asia."

"Going to be a tough choice if it comes to that," I said. "There's always Canada." We sat and finished our beers in silence until Steppenwolf's "Born to be Wild" came on the radio. I turned up the volume, and we sang the chorus and played air guitar along with the instrumentals. We were probably both imagining ourselves slipping across the border to Canada to avoid the draft, letting ourselves believe we were born to be wild.

"Got another beer?" I asked.

"No."

"Want to go do something tomorrow? Maybe help me work on the truck? You could just stay over."

"Works for me. We need to get this rig running if we're going to Canada, eh." We laughed, and when Cher came on the radio singing a sappy ballad, I turned it off and we wandered back to the house.

Mom rousted us out of bed earlier than we wanted, and I loaned David a shirt to wear to church. After a sermon about clean living and obeying our parents, the day was ours to work on the GMC.

"Shit, oh dear," said David, walking around the truck, looking at the damage. "Your brother left you a project."

"Yeah, he had a new Mustang a couple of years ago and he wrecked it too. I think Mom was glad he joined the Marines so he'd quit wrecking cars." I pulled the toolbox out of the back and started working on the broken taillight. David went to work on the fender with a pry bar and a rubber mallet.

"I guess she doesn't feel that way now he's in Vietnam," he said.

"No kidding. She's worried about him, and it pisses me off that he did this. He didn't even wait to get drafted. He just joined up."

I had never taken off a taillight before, so I just started removing screws and stacking pieces on the ground when they came free. Basically, there was the lens (broken) and the housing (bent and rusty) with wires connected to it. The housing was bolted to the fender, and the lens attached to the housing with screws. Soon they were all on the ground with wires hanging out of the fender. I went off to the garage for the taillight I found at a junkyard. When I got back, David had the truck jacked up and was removing the tire so he could reach inside the fender. Installing the new light wasn't hard after I saw how it all went together. I had it done by the time David had beaten the worst of the dent out of the fender.

"Doesn't look half bad," I said, rolling the tire back to the truck and setting it on the lug bolts. "Thanks for your help." It should have been me doing stuff like this with Dad like Joe did, or even me and Joe fixing the truck together like when he helped me build tree forts and fix my bike. Not that I minded David being there, but, like me, he barely knew a crescent wrench from a screwdriver.

David attached the lug nuts and lowered the jack and stowed it in the truck bed. "This shit about your brother. It's got you pissed off, huh?" he said.

"It's not just because I'm against the war either," I said, leaning on the tailgate and wiping my hands on a rag. "It's what it's doing to Mom. I guess me taking a stand against the war kinda has her in a knot too."

David listened to me ramble on while we rounded up tools. Then he lit a cigarette and we folded down the tailgate for a place to sit. "Ain't nothing you can do about it," he said. "You got your own shit. You and your brother will work it out. When he sees you got this truck all fixed up—you'll see. He'll be home safe, and you'll be cruising in this old ride with that brown-eyed girl from the school bus. You gotta have wheels to get lucky, man. That's all that's cramping my style."

"Yeah, maybe." I quit thinking about the bad side of things for a time and let that image hang in my head. I could get a job and fix the truck. I could ask the girl out and maybe go steady. Summer was coming and the hassle of school would be out of the way. That feeling lasted until a few days later when a phone call came, and then nothing was okay again.

SEVEN

I guess it's kinda weird to suddenly fixate on a girl who I'd seen on the bus all year without really noticing. Well, I noticed her—who wouldn't notice a pretty girl—but not like I did now. All year I had been just checking her out, liking the way her ass moved as she walked off the bus in front of me. Now she was part of my new plan: a girl, a job, and some wheels. Those were things I could do something about. As for the war and Mom worrying, I couldn't fix those. They were too big for me, but I could get a date with a girl. Maybe.

Brown Eyes wasn't on the bus Monday morning, and I started making up a scary scenario where her parents took her out of school and I never saw her again. It was silly, but a guy chasing a girl generally doesn't think straight. I had seen David that way many times. Now it was my turn, roaming the halls, looking for a girl without even knowing her name.

In French class, I sat through the torture of programmed lessons with headphones, trying to repeat the sentences from the recorded lesson. *Je m'appelle Jean Leblanc. Mary, tu vas à la bibliothèque?* In the three-minute passing time between French and Algebra 2, I was all eyes for a small, dark-haired girl with freckles, but I might as well have been looking for a ptarmigan in a snowstorm. Then in algebra,

David and I anchored the back row with a couple of stoners who were even less interested in polynomials than I was. "Have you seen that girl?" I asked David.

He played dumb and pretended to be fascinated with completing his calculations. "What girl?"

"Real funny, you turd. She wasn't on the bus. I want to find her before lunch."

We were walking out of class before he grinned and said, "Hey, Barger, I saw that chick from the school bus. She asked about you." He waved and joined the river of students moving up the hall away from me. I gritted my teeth, but I had to laugh. He gave me hope.

I was going through the lunch line for some spaghetti and hot rolls when I spotted her long black hair across the cafeteria. She was in a white blouse and corduroy skirt and sitting by herself, starting on her lunch in a brown paper bag.

"Is this the bad kids' table?" I asked, walking up behind her. I felt like a dumbass not knowing her name. I could just ask her, but I liked the mystery somehow.

"Maybe," she said, flashing a smile and squinting one eye at me critically. "How bad are you?"

"Oh, just a simple anarchist out to overthrow the government."

She laughed. "Well, in that case . . ." I slipped into the seat beside her with my tray of spaghetti.

"I didn't see you on the bus today."

"Yeah, I caught a ride with my dad."

My brain stalled then and I didn't have anything brilliant or sexy to say, so I buttered a roll and took a bite, looking out at the second lunch shift sorting itself into groups like little nations setting up their territories. One table was mostly letter jackets and heads full of hairspray, and there was a table of kids who practically lived in the music room. There were more tables with only Blacks or Natives, and one with grease monkeys who took two periods of shop class so they could work on their cars.

"What are you looking at?" the brown-eyed girl asked, jolting me with an elbow.

"The nations," I said. "Everybody's got their gang in this lunchroom. See, Blacks, Natives, socialites, jocks."

"I guess you're right. Where's your gang?" she asked after a pause to swallow a bite of peanut butter and jelly. We were sharing a table with two boys in chunky sweaters and a couple groping each other under the table and obviously didn't want to be part of any nation but their own.

"No gang for me. Just me and David, a gang of two, but we're a badass gang. You'd fit right in." I took a couple of bites of spaghetti then asked, "So where's your gang? Who do you hang out with?"

She chuckled. "Nobody here, that's for sure. Most of my friends have first lunch, and the others pretty much hang out in the parking lot, not the cafeteria." It figured she'd be hanging with stoners and the hippies, kids I knew from hanging in the back of classrooms.

It made me wonder why she was eating here with me and not her friends. Could it be she came just to see me? Just then, a tall girl in a long denim skirt and a peasant blouse passed the table and said, "Hey, Iris! How's it hangin'?" She didn't wait for an answer. She just moved off into the constant current of people through the cafeteria.

Brown Eyes looked up and said as the girl waved and walked away, "Hey, Janice."

I started laughing and said, "Iris. That's a great name. Iris."

She looked up at me incredulously. "Oh my gosh! You didn't know my name? Oh man! You are terrible! We got sent to high school jail together, and you didn't know my name?" She punched my shoulder, and I winced.

"I was . . . well . . . I was kinda diggin' the mystery." I smiled cautiously, trying to read her reaction.

Iris shook her head and leaned over her lunch sack. "A mystery? Is that what I am? The mystery girl?" Her eyes twinkled and I knew she was playing with me.

"Well, it just got away from me, and then I couldn't figure out how to ask without sounding obvious. Lame, huh?" I went back to work on my pile of spaghetti.

"You didn't want to sound *obviously* what?"

"Quit that. You know what I mean." I was feeling the conversation going downhill, and I didn't want that. I wanted to spend more time with Iris, not less, and I now couldn't tell if she was irritated or teasing. I put all my money on one play. "Actually, this is great timing because I wanted to ask you out, and I couldn't if I didn't know your name. I mean, how would that look?"

She just kept playing with her food and not saying much. No, she wasn't saying anything. Around us the hum of conversation and the rattle of food trays roared in my ears. I wished David would show up and break the silence, but he was washing dishes in the kitchen. I was on my own. "So? So, do you want to go out with me?" I finally said. I couldn't look at her, so I stared at the hand-printed pep rally posters left from last week.

"On a date?"

This was becoming painful, and she wasn't helping. "Yeah, I guess. Yeah, a date," I said.

"Oh Sam, that is so sweet and so square. A date, really? "

"Well, I thought, you know. We fought The Man together, and you know . . . Oh crap, you are killing me, woman. Sure, a date, why not?"

"Why not?" she repeated. " 'Cause it's not my thing—dating, I mean. First a date, then you'll be asking me to the prom, and I'm just not into all that Cinderella and Prince Charming charade. You're really sweet, Sam, but if that's what you want, I'm the wrong girl."

She finally put down her sandwich and took a breath. I noticed she didn't eat the bones. There were crusts of homemade bread stacked on the corner of the paper sandwich bag.

"Whoa. Who said anything about the prom?"

Just when she was about to speak the bell rang, and she rolled her eyes in irritation. "Sam, it's just, well, I thought we were buds just hanging together. And I don't want to date anybody. Can't I just be in your gang?" She got soft and tender eyed. "I'm sorry, Sam. Really." Then she smiled. "But. I'm really glad you know my name now."

I was at a loss, so I reached over and took one of her sandwich bones and shoved it in my mouth instead of my foot. "I love peanut butter and raspberry jam," I said, a dumbass thing to say, but I was in over my head and floundering.

Before I could say more, she pushed the paper with the sandwich bones in front of me and walked away, and I was sitting alone in the cafeteria as it slowly emptied and grew quiet. I couldn't believe she hit me with the I-just-want-to-be-friends line; that's not how I saw things going. I saw us holding hands in the hall, snuggling on the bus together, making out in the GMC. It pissed me off that she got to me that way, but she did. Just buds, she said. I had David. I didn't need another buddy.

EIGHT

The note on the door of Polar Pizza read *HELP WANTED, INQUIRE WITHIN.* I stepped closer and peered through the glass door. Inside the pizza parlor, a girl in a brown waitress's uniform was running a vacuum. At first she didn't hear when I knocked, and I could only watch her move about the dining room. Her motions were loose and graceful, like she was dancing with the Hoover, and I could hear the thump of the Rolling Stones in the background. Instead of knocking again, I just watched the bouncing red ponytail and rounded hips that rocked across the room in time to the music.

Having struck out with Iris, I had moved on to Stage Two and Three of my plan: a job and some wheels. I needed money to get the '57 Jimmy running like I had promised Joe. Putting a starter in couldn't be that hard if I had the money for it, and even fixing the fenders wouldn't be impossible. I definitely needed to get a job though, and right then I wanted *this* job. *To hell with Iris,* I thought. I'd clean toilets all day to be around the girl with the vacuum. By the time she opened the door and showed me her bright-green eyes, I didn't want to work anyplace but the Polar Pizza.

"Hi, I bet you're here about the job," she said, opening the door and stepping back to invite me in. She was small. Mom would have said petite, but she still had all the parts—breasts, legs, hips, lips, and eyes I couldn't turn away from.

I tried to play it cool, but my tongue was suddenly thick and dry. "Yeah. I saw the sign."

"I'm Julie. You need to talk to my dad." Then over her shoulder and louder, "Dad, another victim!" She laughed and turned back to me. "He's nice. You'll like working for him." I grinned at the way she said it like I already had the job.

A round, freckled man in a T-shirt and white sailor cap came through the batwing doors from the kitchen and grabbed my hand. "My name is Sam, Sam Barger," I said.

"Pete Parelli. Come have the tour." He led me to the kitchen. "This could be your big break, Sam. There's a lotta dough to be made in the pizza business." He laughed at his pun. I chuckled, and he handed me a paper plate with a slice of pizza.

"I wanted to call the place Pete Parelli's Polar Pizza Parlor," he said. "But Julie said that was too much, so I dropped the Pete Parelli. Then she dropped the Parlor." I took a bite off my plate. His pizza was better than his jokes—a lot better. We walked through the yellow building, a small cinder block cube that was half kitchen and half dining room divided by a wall with batwing doors and a pickup window about chest high. Six tables with chairs and red-checkered tablecloths were scattered around the dining room surrounded by fake walnut paneling, like in a trailer house. The decorations consisted of framed pictures of old Italian buildings and Julie. She had stopped vacuuming and was wiping down tables, and I kept stealing peeks at the backs of her legs as she reached and twisted and stretched so that the hem of her short waitress uniform moved up and down her thigh.

I could concentrate better when Pete led me into the kitchen where the pizza oven was pushing the temperature up past comfortable. "And here is your office," said Pete with a sweeping gesture that took in three big sinks and stainless shelves full of pots and pans. "Keep the place clean and tidy, show up for work, and don't piss me off," he said. "Do that, and I'll teach you to make pizza so good the girls will be following you home at night." He laughed. "There's a lotta dough to be made in the pizza business," Pete said for the second time, and I laughed like I'd never heard it before because I wanted to stay there amid the smell of garlic, dough, and tomato sauce.

There was more here at Polar Pizza than the pretty girl in the dining room and the money to fix the '57. The place felt warm, foreign, and inviting like I thought a beach in Hawaii would. I could use a dose of that, so the next day after school, I was at the Polar Pizza like a coyote on a moose kill. From then on, I worked three days a week. Pete said that come summer I'd be full time, if he didn't fire me. There was no way I was going blow a chance at spending my evenings smelling Italian flavors and drooling over a redheaded girl named Julie, even if she was out of my league.

From the first day on the job, Pete taught me the different ingredients in pizza and showed me how to work the dough into the flat circles that became the crust. Every day I scrubbed the toilet, washed dishes, took out the trash, and cleaned the kitchen. When I wasn't mopping floors, stocking supplies, or washing dishes, I was shredding cheese, mixing dough, or stirring the sauce that Pete made from canned tomatoes, garlic, and herbs. He simmered it for several hours with a ham bone in it, a secret I had to swear not to reveal.

Some days I would be elbow deep in dishwashing and Pete would yell, "Leave that pearl diving and come learn some cooking." Then he'd teach me another trick of the trade. By the third week, I had memorized the meatball recipe and knew the ingredients of most of the pizzas on the menu.

Julie said that fishing was Pete's real motive for teaching me so fast. "He wants you to be able to run the kitchen by the end of June so he can go salmon fishing once a week. I can run the place, but he thinks only a man can make pizza."

I didn't care about his motivation. Pete made me feel like just another guy, and the things he taught me made me feel competent and strong. And, yeah, there was probably something in me looking for a father figure, but in the spring of 1968 Polar Pizza was better than home and school any way I looked at it. If it put money in my pocket, pearl diving was just fine with me. Besides, the scenery was incredible.

NINE

At school we were all suffering through the last weeks of spring semester, trying to do as little homework as possible. The snow was gone and the rush of green and sunlight brought the promise of summer into our world. Everyone's parents were excited about the discovery of oil on the North Slope of Alaska, scared about the Black Panthers, and excited about Richard Nixon. Of course, Iris and I hoped Bobby Kennedy would be the Democratic candidate who could beat Nixon and end the war. Then, just when I was starting to pay attention and knew who Martin Luther King, Jr. was, he got assassinated.

"I can't believe it," Iris said. "Martin Luther King is dead." We were sitting at a party she had invited me to. *Not a date*, she insisted, but she wore a nice dress like it was a date, and we were together. I would take what I could get. The party was a bunch of family station wagons and ten-year-old sedans parked in a gravel pit. One guy had a '62 Chevy with a new cassette player and four speakers blasting the Rolling Stones, and some kids were dancing on a flat stretch of gravel between the cars.

"Can you believe it?" I said. "Who shoots a preacher? Nobody's safe anymore." Iris and I were sitting in the open back of a Buick station wagon passing a bottle of Boone's Farm wine back and forth.

"It's a revolution, Sam," she said, "and there are people who don't want things to change. They don't want Blacks to be equal, they don't want kids speaking their minds, and they want us women to stay in the kitchen and keep our mouths shut. But it's going to happen, Sam."

"I knew you'd get that women's lib bit in there," I said. I did feel kind of guilty because while she was talking about women's liberation, I was checking out her exposed thighs peeking out from the hem of her short denim dress. She might want to be *just buds*, but I hadn't given up on changing her mind. The wine was working on me by then and I couldn't resist a joke. "We don't want women in the kitchen all the time. We like you in the bedroom too."

She punched my shoulder. "You're a sexist pig," she said, but we both laughed. We'd been hanging out together a lot, talking about the peace movement and news on the war. I discovered that we both liked Buffalo Springfield and the Moody Blues, and thought the Beatles were overrated. I might have a bit of a crush on Julie at Polar Pizza, but when I was around Iris, I got stirred up in a whole different way.

"You don't really mean that, do you? About women? We should be able to work if we want just like men. What about your mom? She works, right?" Iris asked.

I took a pull at the bottle and thought back to when Mom didn't work. "She didn't always. Back when Dad was alive, she was all homemade bread and PTA. Now she has to work."

"See. Your mom's out there leading the charge for women."

"Yeah, but not because she wants to. She says she'd trade her job for it all to be back how it was with Dad bringing home the paychecks. She says that anyway, but I think it's because she misses Dad. She likes working and being a boss. Don't try and tell her she's not equal."

"I knew you were a smart guy," Iris said, and she leaned against my shoulder. I could smell the herbal cologne she wore—sandalwood, I think, a fragrance like a forest. I wanted to touch her hair and feel her soft cheek.

The evening was bright but cool, and I felt her shiver when a breeze blew down from the mountains and stirred the dust in the gravel pit. I reached behind and pulled a blanket around her shoulders. She looked up and smiled. "Thanks," she said. There was still enough day left to see her eyes, and they invited me, so I put my arm around her blanketed shoulder and kissed her.

And she kissed me back! Her hand reached up to the back of my head to make the kiss last. We kissed long and softly, then she opened her mouth and our tongues touched and suddenly the evening wasn't cold anymore. I wrapped the blanket around us anyway and pretended no one else was in our world. I tasted her neck where the fragrance of sandalwood was strong and found her mouth again.

"You want to lie down?" I whispered.

"Don't push your luck, Barger." But her eyes twinkled, and we kept kissing. I could feel the wine and the passion working on me, and it was all I could do not reach for her breasts or stroke her bare legs. *Don't push your luck, Barger* seemed like good advice right then.

I don't know how long we were making out in the back of that station wagon, but I suddenly realized that the music had stopped and most of the cars were either gone or silent with steamed-up windows. We caught a ride home, and I was left with only the smell of the girl on my shirt and the taste of her kisses, which wasn't bad for not going on a date. I was smart enough to know, however, that the siege of Iris wasn't over, and there was a good chance that Monday she would still insist on being just friends. What I didn't know was that things were about to get crazy and I was going to need all the friendship I could get.

TEN

Two weeks before summer vacation, a taxicab brought Joe home again, back from the war. The door of the cab opened, and a pair of crutches came poking out. Then came one leg, then the other. Joe paused with one hand on the car door and his butt still on the seat. He was lean and pale. For a moment I thought it wasn't Joe at all. He heaved himself out with a grimace and looked at me with his crooked smile. "You need a haircut, punk. You still tryin' to be one of those hippie war protesters?" He laughed, but he didn't know how right he was.

I put my hand on the hair that now had grown long enough to cover my ears and said, "Hey, brother." The driver handed me a duffel and a canvas grip.

Mom grabbed Joe and almost knocked him down, clutching at him while he hobbled to the house on his crutches. They waddled up to the house like a three-legged horse, but I didn't laugh and let Mom have her moment with Joe.

That first night home, Joe lay sideways on the bed and lit a cigarette. "Dig into that duffel, Humpy. See if I've got a bottle in there," he said.

I opened the duffel and rummaged through socks and underwear until I found a pint of whiskey. "What's it like?" I asked. "The war, I mean."

"I thought you meant this." Joe gestured with the bottle, then he snapped the seal and took a long pull. He handed it to me open and I tipped it up and tasted fire. I tried not to show how the liquor burned my mouth and throat, but my eyes watered, so I knew he could tell. When I handed back the bottle, he nodded his approval and took a swallow.

He squinted through the smoke of his cigarette and laughed. "What was it like? Hot, wet. Sticky and damn hot. Eating slop, sleeping in the mud, or worse. Or not eatin' or sleepin' at all." He paused and took another pull on the bottle. "And that was the good part."

He tried to roll over on his back, but I could see that hurt too much, so he turned back to his side and took another hit off the bottle. He didn't offer it to me. He just held it while he stared at the wall. "I shot a water buffalo with a grenade launcher." He laughed like a movie villain. "There wasn't enough left to make a meatloaf. And my buddy, Frank—you'll meet him—he liked shootin' rats. No shit, Sam, those rats were big as cats, and ol' Frank—there's a crazy sumbitch—he'd shoot 'em with a .45 automatic for hours. He was a hunting fool for them rats."

I laughed, but I went to bed confused. Joe was acting like he was just on a weird sort of vacation with a bunch of other guys. He didn't talk about how he got shot or what the war was really like. The Viet Cong were never mentioned that night, like they weren't even part of the experience. He fell asleep with a cigarette in one hand and the bottle in the other. I took them out of his hands, snuffed the cigarette, and corked the bottle of whiskey, but I left it by his bed.

In the morning, the bottle was gone, and when I looked out the window I could see Joe hobbling out to the '57. He lifted the hood and leaned on his crutches as he peered into the open mouth of the engine compartment. I poured coffee for both of us from the electric percolator and walked out to join him, leaving a brown trail of spilled coffee leading from the back door to the truck.

"Thanks for the coffee, kid," said Joe. "Next time bring a whole cup." He nodded at the spilled coffee.

I hung my arms on the truck fender, letting the steaming coffee fill my nose and waiting for something I couldn't identify. "Sorry I didn't get it running yet," I said. "But I pounded out the dent in that fender and . . ."

"What happened . . . besides nothin'?" Joe sipped the coffee and lifted the cup in salute.

I looked at the empty metal tray waiting for a battery and the loose wires that still needed to be connected to the battery posts. "I didn't have the money and I figured there wasn't no hurry."

"Yeah, well, I got no wheels now." Joe leaned on the fender and shook his head. "If you want something, kid, you gotta put out some effort. This wasn't a big thing." He drank the coffee in one swallow and set the cup aside. He was pale and sickly looking, nothing like the fit, tan soldier who had left the house a few months ago.

I knew he was right and I could have gotten more done, but I wasn't ready to admit it. "I know. I didn't have any money. But I'm going to now that I'm working." I leaned in and wiped the dust off the air cleaner with my bare hand. "Okay, here's the deal. It didn't seem worth the trouble since Mom won't let me drive, and besides, I didn't think you'd be home this soon."

Joe shook a cigarette out of the pack and lit it. "Gee, Sam. Sorry I got shot in the ass and ruined your plans."

"We can fix it together." I couldn't help feeling guilty for letting him down. There was a time when we could just naturally work together like we did building a tree fort when I wanted one, or when we'd wash the Mustang together and change the oil and plugs. That's how I had learned most of what I knew about fixing things. Instead, we were butting heads.

"Well, crap, Joe, you didn't have to wreck it in the first place. You screwed me both ways, you know."

"What do you mean? Mom won't let you drive because of me?" He was laughing now. And that really pissed me off. He turned his back to the wind and leaned on his crutches while he lit a cigarette.

"She won't. She said I have to wait another year to get my license when I've got, as she says, 'a level head on my shoulders.' You know how she is. With you wrecking the Mustang and the truck. Shit, I never had a chance." The truck hood gaped like an open mouth with something to say.

"You don't need your mom to get a driver's license, idiot. You just go take the test and get it. Christ! This is a real snafu. Shit!" Joe slammed the hood closed, and the coffee cup bounced onto the ground. We stood in the crisp morning with the cold steel of the GMC truck between us. Then Joe grabbed his crutches and lurched his way back to the house. That whole thing must have worn him out because he clumped off back to bed.

I stayed and cleaned up the broken mug and messed around with the truck, fixing the loose latch on the tailgate and sweeping leaves and trash out of the bed. I wondered the whole time about Joe and how he'd changed. Maybe it was the wound. When Dad had his first heart attack, he'd had been moody and easy to set off too. Maybe that's what it was with Joe, I told myself. But I really thought it was the war. It was the goddamn war.

The next night when we were alone in the bedroom again and Joe was sober, I said, "Tell me about the war, Joe. What's battle really like?"

"Are you serious?" He was folding his laundry and stowing it Marine style. Square corners and tidy stacks. "Imagine it's a hundred degrees and you're sitting in a dark outhouse hole full of shit with mortars, grenades, and rifle fire blasting the holy hell out of your outhouse. That's what it's like. It's called 'in the shit' for a reason."

"How'd you stand that?"

"We just did. Or we didn't. Some guys didn't. Why don't you square away your crap on the floor? Mom's been slacking off on you, I see."

I looked at the dirty underwear and socks littering the floor around my bed and shook my head. "Anything to make you happy, big brother." Then I was stacking and stowing too, but there were no folds or square corners on my side of the room. Instead, I started talking about moose hunting. I'd been thinking about it since Joe had left, and the idea had grown on me. "You know, Joe," I said, "we can go hunting now, now that you're home."

"Yeah, I guess so, if we had a truck that ran and I didn't have these crutches. Hunting's so easy on crutches, ya know." He shook a cigarette out the pack, lit it, and fell back on the bed.

I sat on the bed and studied my brother sprawled out looking at the ceiling. "No, when you're healed. When you're better. You'll be good by then, right? By moose season, I mean."

Joe was silent, blowing smoke rings like Dad used to, little gray donuts of smoke that rose and twisted until they were just thinning wisps against the ceiling. "Did I tell you about hunting water buffalo with grenade launchers?"

"Last night you told me, and about the rats too."

"The rats, oh yeah, the rats. They were worse than the Viet Cong. If that's possible. Big as cats. I can't count how many of them we blasted."

I wanted to tell him that I'd read about the Viet Cong and how they were just fighting for their country like the colonists in the Revolution. But it didn't seem like the time. "What are they like? The Viet Cong?"

"The Gooks? Nasty little men in black pajamas. No shit. Mean as hell, those little devils. They did this to me, Sam. Shot me in the leg and the ass, then killed two of my buddies the same day. Hell of a deal." That was the last he said before he started snoring.

I finished clearing my laundry and then turned off the light and lay in the dark, thinking of being in the war, knowing that men were hiding in the hot, wet jungle trying to kill me, maybe watching a friend like David die. I remembered being a little kid afraid of the dark. Dad had expected me to tough it out, denying me even an open door at bedtime to let a little light in the bedroom. So I had trembled in the pitch darkness of winter nights. Joe would lie in bed and talk to me, telling me stories until I fell asleep. If I woke in the night with nightmares, he'd crawl under my covers and lie next to me until I fell asleep again. To experience that darkness with an actual threat of death lurking in it was beyond my imagination.

I picked up a Mickey Spillane novel and tried to leave reality behind. For an hour I read, then killed the light.

Halfway through the night, I was blasted awake by a scream and thud from across the room.

"Incoming! Take cover!"

I leaped up. "Joe! You okay?"

He lay on the floor, kicking and lashing out with his hands. "Cover your ass!" he yelled.

Mom ran in from her room. "Joseph, Joseph! Oh my God! Are you okay? What is it?"

Joe crawled under the bed, clutching his pillow to his chest. He didn't seem to hear us talking to him. He just thrashed and beat against the bed and the floor and the wall. I looked at Mom standing there in her nightgown and curlers with her hand over her mouth.

"Joe. Joe?" She went toward him slowly, kneeling down to him, speaking softly. "Joe, it's okay, Joe. You're safe." Then she went firm and loud. "Joe! Wake up, Joe. Wake up!"

His eyes opened, and he stared at us like he didn't know us. Mom reached for him like he was a five-year-old suffering the night terrors. His eyes went wide then clenched closed, squinted tight. His face was all flushed like he had a fever. I could see the fear in him. I could see it clear as day. All the while he was sweating and shivering, and I'm not sure he recognized us. I looked at Mom, but she had that all-business, my-kid-needs-me look, and there wasn't room in that to answer my questions. Finally, Joe just lay back on the floor and sobbed. Yes, he was crying, and I felt embarrassed to watch such a thing.

We eventually got him back in bed, and he seemed okay except now his wound hurt, so he had to have a pain pill. That seemed to make him restless. He sat up the rest of the night in the living room smoking cigarettes and talking to himself—or maybe it was ghosts he was talking to. The whole thing had me wide awake, and I lay in bed staring out the window wondering what the hell was going on.

ELEVEN

Joe's first week home was full of nightmares, couch sleeping, and arguments about my long hair and my lack of respect for authority, meaning him. I wandered around trying to figure out why Joe talked all cool and tough during the day and then at night he cried and screamed like a little kid. We didn't talk about the war.

"What's going on with Joe?" I asked Mom one day when we were alone.

"It's warfare, son. It's hard on men. Harder than you and I can imagine. He just needs time. You'll see. Just be his brother and be patient. He'll come around." She got up then and went to her bedroom. I couldn't figure out if she was lying to me or to herself.

All this turmoil kept me from wanting to talk to anyone, but that night after Mom went to bed and I had some privacy, I called Iris. "What are you doing?" I asked, not knowing how else to start a conversation.

"Reading."

"What are you reading?"

"You'll laugh if I told you." Her voice was softer and younger on the phone. I wanted her to talk so I could just listen to the music of it.

"I wouldn't laugh . . . not much anyway. Come on, what are you reading? *Little Women*?"

She giggled, and I loved that sound. It was what I needed. "Okay, I'm reading *The Feminine Mystique.* Go ahead and laugh."

I did. "Isn't that like the manifesto of the women's movement? Men are jerks and all that?"

Iris sighed. "She doesn't say men are jerks, but they can be when they expect us to be their housemaids and whores. It's really about women being able to be all the things men are. That they don't have to be just housewives."

"Got it."

"You sound skeptical. Look at your mom. She works just like a man every day and is still your mom. We should be your equals with all the same choices."

"Okay," I said, "I can deal with that." And with a clumsy segue, I said, "Want to hang out this weekend? We could go see *Planet of the Apes*?"

I could hear her breathing on the other end of the line, and my heart raced. "Oh that sounds great, I want to see that movie, but I'm going to Dad's camp this weekend. He's setting up for summer and I need to help. Then when school's out I'm going there for the summer."

I couldn't feel anything for the moment except disappointment and jealousy. Her dad was a fishing guide, and working out on some wilderness lodge sounded a lot more adventuresome than cooking pizzas. "That sounds really great," I said. "I would love to get away for the summer. Doesn't your dad need a camp cook?"

"You mean you make more than pizza?"

I chuckled. "Are you kidding? If I can't make it, I can fake it." I leaned back on the couch, starting to relax a bit.

"Oh really? I don't think you'd want my job. I'm the cook, maid, outboard mechanic, and tourist nursemaid," she said with a laugh. "Not as exciting as it sounds."

"Doesn't sound very liberated."

"Not very, but Dad's cool to work for."

"More fun than living with Joe right now," I said. I hadn't meant to say anything about Joe, but it just came out.

"Isn't he getting better?"

"Oh he's healing fine physically, but his head is pretty messed up. Just one more bad thing about the war." That's all I wanted to say. Everything was so damn complicated and personal that I didn't even know how to talk about it, so I let it drop. The phone was silent as we sat on our words, breathing in each other's ears. It wasn't something easy to talk about, and Joe would claim he was just readjusting and blowing off steam. But sometimes when he talked, I wondered if there was any of the old Joe left at all.

"Sam, I'm so sorry," Iris said. I'm not sure there was more to be said than that, but her dad told her to get off the phone anyway.

I sat by the phone for a time and then tried the TV, but the stations were off the air for the night. I had nowhere to hide from the fever Joe had spread. Even the simplest of conversations would set him off.

Once at dinner, Joe and I were eating pork chops and fried potatoes across from each other. Mom said, "So, Joe, why don't you give Sam a hand getting his pickup truck running? Sam could do the work you can't get to yet, and you could show him how."

Joe laughed then snarled, "His truck? The '57 is mine. I already got a battery for it. Now I need a starter."

"You gave it to me!" I growled around a mouthful of potatoes, and the fight was on.

"There was a condition, Humpy," Joe said. "You were supposed to get it running." I winced. I had liked when Dad called me Humpy, a name I got for being small like the pink salmon, but Joe only used it when he was feeling superior, like I was just a little punk. "You don't get somethin' for nothin', kid. It's time you learned that."

"Why, so you could come home and drive it when you want to?" I spat.

"Well, no one's driving it now, Humpy." There it was again. Calling me Humpy to put me down and make me feel small. "You must've used all your money at the barbershop." Joe pointed his fork at me. "You better get a haircut before somebody comes along and cuts it for you."

"Can you two talk without fighting?" Mom asked. Slammed strawberry rhubarb pie down in front of us, but it was like she wasn't even in the room.

"I'd like to see 'em try!" I growled. There he went with the hair again. He couldn't see that guys like me grew our hair because we could, so we wouldn't look like straight-laced, follow-orders suckers like him, and I didn't feel like trying to explain it.

"Ooh! A tough guy! I thought you hippies were all about peace and love." He waved a peace sign in my face, and I slapped it away. "You know what us jarheads call that peace symbol you hippies are all so proud of? The track of the great American chicken."

I swept up his plate and fork and headed to the sink to start the dishes.

"Sorry, Mom. I don't feel like pie right now," I said loudly. "Screw you, Joe! I'm not a hippie. I'm not out panhandling for spare change. I just wear my hair how I like it. You think you look cool with your stupid Marine crew cut?"

"Samuel!" Mom barked. "You two will be the death of me."

Joe tried to leap to his feet, and Mom slapped her hands on the table. "You boys stop it this instant! I won't have this in my kitchen. Joe, you go cool off, and Sam, you get those dishes done. There are more important things than how long a man's hair is. Now you two need to work this out. Sam, I think your hair is a sight, and Joseph, you need to heal up before you think about crawling around under that truck."

I couldn't resist being a jerk. "Yeah, like he had no business going off to fight in a stupid war that's none of our business. You're a sucker, Joe, a sucker to fall for their bull."

"That what they teach you in school?" he said. "A stupid war? We fight wars over there so we don't have to fight them here! You think the Chinese will stop in 'Nam? No sir. And that's our line in the sand!" He hobbled off and slammed the bedroom door.

All my arguments always felt weak and empty against Joe's confidence. My brother seemed so sure while for me, nothing seemed sure. I tuned the kitchen radio to a rock station and lost myself in soapsuds and the whine of electric guitar and pumping drums. Down the short hallway, Joe turned up the radio so the twang of country music came from the bedroom we shared. The Bargers' charming bungalow was getting small, and I was feeling like I was trapped in an outhouse with a wolverine.

Twice we ended up toe to toe in the center of the bedroom. The first time, Joe had walked in when I was playing a *Cream* album and said, "What is that crap?" He turned off the record player. Mom had to break us up that time. The second time, she wasn't around when I came home from school and found Joe drunk in the middle of the afternoon.

"How was school today, comrade?" he mocked.

"We practiced overthrowing the government and burning Bibles. I got an A."

"That's not funny."

"I was just joking," I said, realizing that he was in no mood for my bullshit. "I'm going out."

"To the barber, maybe?" A cigarette hung from the corner of Joe's mouth, and his eye squinted against the smoke like a bad James Dean.

"I ain't getting a haircut, you son-of-a-bitch. Get used to it!"

"Watch your mouth."

"I don't need some drunk asshole telling me how to talk, Joe. Shove it!"

Joe stood up and smacked my shoulder. "You wanna start something? Come on!"

"Forget it. Just leave me alone!" I should have shut my big mouth and left, but who does that when they're really pissed off?

"Come on! Are you some kind of candy-ass? Hit me!" Even on crutches, Joe was across the room before I could blink.

"No."

"Come on! I'll give you the first punch."

Suddenly, I was as psycho as he was. I forgot about him being wounded and on crutches. I didn't even know I was doing it when I hit him in the face. There was no thought, just my fist.

Joe fell back onto the bed, but he came up quickly, ignoring his bad leg. He slapped me on the side of the head with his open hand, and it rang like a bell. Then he came with a backhand to the other side. I staggered and put up my hands. I didn't go down though. No way I was going to let him knock me off my feet. Ever. I bailed then, from the room, from this brother, from the shame of my tears. I slammed out the back door feeling weak and stupid. A sixteen-year-old kid fighting a Marine, wounded or not, was asking to get a broken nose, or worse.

TWELVE

The clock on the wall above the stack of pizza boxes read 10:55, and I was at the soda machine drawing a 7Up and a root beer. "Hey, slowpoke! You about ready to open?" I called.

"Born ready!" came Julie's reply, and her face appeared around the corner. "All I need is a man who knows how to cook," she said with a giggle and a swing of her hips.

I extended the 7Up through the order window. "Then lady, you got everything you need right here. I am a pizza-cookin' machine." I was suddenly a great force of will, as bold as my brother and father.

"A machine, is it?" she asked in mock amazement, sipping her 7Up through a straw and laughing with her eyes.

"I am the pizza-matic with my dough a-risin', and I just hope your little ass can keep up."

"Oh, Sam. Is that your dough a-risin'?" she said in a high-pitched Southern twang. "Oh my word."

I looked away blushing, then turned back to watch her parade across the dining room. She twirled her apron over her head then stood at the door swinging her hips as she tied the apron strings. She flipped the sign for *CLOSED* to *OPEN* and unlocked the deadbolt. Polar Pizza was open.

For a moment I hung frozen in place like I did when watching a loon dancing across a fog-draped pond or a moose crossing a frosty muskeg. Julie in her brown waitress uniform was like a thrush flitting about in a forest thicket, and I admired the energy that she put into that constant motion. I realized I'd never seen her in anything but her brown zippered uniform dress that she came and left in every day. I drank the root beer, letting the bubbles wash through me, tickling my throat. I imagined her in a plaid skirt and white blouse like some of the girls were wearing now. Or, even better, a pair of cutoffs and a braless T-shirt. I wondered if I'd ever get the courage to do more than just stare at her and joke around from the safety of my cook station.

The days when Pete went fishing usually started this way—with a pause for a drink, me teasing, and Julie flirting as we made the place ready for business. I had to think that she enjoyed those days when just the two of us made the place hum. Julie sold the pizzas, poured the drinks, and generally managed the place while I handled the kitchen. Sometimes she did Pizza Pete imitations to remind me that she was boss. "Where's that pearl diver? Those dishes ain't getting cleaner just sitting there," she called.

"Yeah, boss," I answered, "I'm all over it."

I started my day by prepping toppings and cooking off meatballs for the meatball sandwiches. While the meatballs baked in the oven, I built a big bowl of Pete's signature salad and laid out my workstation. Lined up in order on the cold table were stainless bins of shredded cheese, crumbles of sausage, slices of pepperoni and ham, black olives, green peppers, anchovies, mushrooms, and the other toppings to make a dozen varieties of pizza. I stirred the sauce on the stove and let the garlic-tomato air wash around me. All the while I was grating cheese and dicing peppers, Julie flitted in and out of my view like a songbird in a garden, catching my eye with the twist of her hips or a toss of her hair pulled back into a ponytail.

Lunch business soon picked up to a steady flow, with a trickle of takeout pizza in the afternoon. Then couples and groups started coming in for sit-down dinner. It would slow again after that until the Fireweed Theater down the street let out. We'd be slammed for about an hour with people hungry after the movie.

I liked the challenge of busy days when I was working multiple orders at a time—tossing, rolling, saucing, and cheesing in a cadence that worked like a close-order drill. Cheese, sausage, Canadian bacon, and pepperoni pizzas were the regulars. I split French rolls and filled them with meatballs, sauce, and cheese and slid them in the oven. I tossed the famous Pete's salad in woven wood bowls, and made cheese breadsticks by rolling out pizza dough and slicing it into finger-sized pieces sprinkled with garlic, oil, and parmesan.

When Polar Pizza was rockin' and rollin', Julie and I kept our banter lively all evening. "Shall I just tell those people waiting for two pizzas and a salad to go somewhere else?" Julie would ask.

I would look serious and reply, "Oh, was that order for today?"

Sometimes just for fun, I would bake a pizza dough with no toppings and call, "Order up!" and wait to see how far Julie would go with it before spotting the trick. Once, she delivered it all the way to the table. The whole place laughed over that one. It was easy for my imagination to get the best of me on nights like that when it felt we were the only ones in on a private little joke, and I would forget we were just joking.

I felt guilty about flirting with Julie like I was cheating on Iris, and maybe I was, but I wasn't sure what I had going with Iris, and whatever we had seemed so fragile it might not last the summer. Just when I thought I was getting somewhere with Iris, she was off to spend the summer working with her dad at some lake a hundred miles away. We weren't going steady, having sex, or even holding hands in the hall, but we hung out, made out, and smoked a joint before she left. She wrote her address on an index card that she folded and slipped into the pocket of my Levi's jacket. She patted the pocket and said, "Write me, big guy."

"Yeah, maybe," I said, like I didn't care one way or another, but I buttoned the flap on my jacket pocket and smiled. Of course, I wrote to her as soon as she left. Not a long letter—just a note, really—talking about work and how the death of Bobby Kennedy had changed our world. I told her I had found a starter for the truck and how when she returned I would have wheels. That didn't matter much to her, I figured, but she knew it was on my list of shit to get done. I didn't write about Polar Pizza for reasons obvious to me and perhaps no one else.

One evening I was taking the trash to the dumpster in the alley and nearly walked into a big Plymouth hardtop with big rear fins and a long hood. Julie was leaning against the driver's door with a cigarette in her hand. I hadn't seen her smoking before. Her arms formed an L shape with one arm crossing beneath her breasts and that hand supporting the elbow of her cigarette hand. Is this what they mean by "smoking-hot babe"? I've seen lots of women hold that pose like cigarettes were heavy and the smoking arm needed extra bracing. I never saw men do it.

"Sam, come meet my husband, Mike," she said.

The word "husband" hung in the air like a cartoon word bubble. Husband! I tried not to act surprised. *Pow!* I tried not to act like I was in shock. *Bam!* I tried not to give away my disappointment. A husband? *Crack!*

"Hey," I said, walking toward the car with my muscles tightening like I was about to crap my pants. The guy didn't look much older than me, but he had short hair and a slender mustache that said he was a GI.

Husband? A little part of me wanted to say, *What the hell? You have a husband? Aren't you just a teenager like me? You can't have a husband!* I wanted to say all that to her. No, I wanted to yell it at her. But I just stood there and said, "All right, your husband. Hey, Mike. Nice to meet you." I shook his hand. It was slender and long.

When I went back into work, I couldn't remember what the husband looked like and realized I was embarrassed, like I had been doing something wrong. Mom would say it was a sin to lust after a married woman, but how was I supposed to know she was married?

That night the orders were steady so that both me and Julie were hot and sweaty when she brought me an ice water not long before closing time. She leaned on the doorframe, half in the kitchen, with sweat glistening on the exposed V of her cleavage and dotting her forehead. "I love it like this," she said. "We are kicking ass and taking names, Big Sam." We toasted with our water cups, and I realized that she was much smaller than me. It helped me forget that she was older and married. She had told me that she graduated the year before, so she had to be nineteen. "We're a good team," she said.

I was flushed red with the heat of the pizza ovens, but she made me flush even hotter, married or not. *We're a good team* kept ringing in my ears. I was excited like we were making out in the backseat of a car up on Baxter Road, and she wasn't married and I wasn't a young dreamer.

"Right on!" I blurted. Then I turned back to my pizzas. I flipped open a pizza oven and in one motion pulled a large pepperoni from the oven and slid it onto the wooden cutting board. The other hand was already reaching for the twenty-inch French knife that followed the pizza to the board. "Order up!" And the pizza twirled into the pickup window.

Julie was still in the doorway with her figure silhouetted by the evening sunlight passing through her dress. "I love to watch you work."

I didn't say what I was thinking.

She took the pizza and was back soon with a fresh order. "Let's rush this so we can get these guys out of here." I hadn't checked the clock, but I knew we were coming up on closing time. She nodded at a table of three men in the corner. "That's why Dad won't serve beer."

"What's up?" I asked her. The three guys were laughing and shuffling chairs at the table by the door. They were loud and silly the way beer can make you.

Julie waved it off. "Just a little grabby and crude, that's all. Nothing I can't handle." She scooped up a tray of drinks and floated across the room. While I made the pizza, I watched as the guys talked trash and tried to put hands on Julie, but she danced out of their reach and still managed to serve their iced teas and sodas. She shook her head and pursed her lips when one called across the room, "Hey sweetie, when does the floor show start?"

One guy was husky and rough looking in a worn fatigue jacket, while the others were young and familiar looking in bell-bottom jeans and T-shirts. Julie went about serving the other two tables of customers, giving them extra attention to avoid the drunks. I bristled when I recognized Jacob Phelps, who had hit Iris with soggy napkins in the cafeteria during our peace protest, and his sidekick Bobby Carson, two guys I couldn't forget. When a fourth fellow showed up, I knew him too. It was Joe.

I felt the heat run up my back, so I turned and checked the pizzas, but there was only an order of cheese bread I'd made for the end of the day. When I looked up, Julie was slipping past me to the back of the kitchen, and one group of customers was leaving. Suddenly Joe was leaning in the pickup window. "Hey ya, Sam! Where'd that cute little waitress go? Made me jump to see you here. Forgot this was where you worked. Where'd our little gal go, I want some service . . . if you know what I mean."

I ignored him as I put the last of the toppings on their pizza and sprinkled it with cheese. I could smell the liquor and saw the drunken squint in Joe's eye. "She's gone on break," I lied. I slid the pie into the oven. Building the pizza had calmed me some, but now my hands were empty. I grabbed a rag and wiped the stainless steel counter, my hand moving in repetitive circles across the clean countertop.

"Does that mean she's waiting out back for me, hoping for me to make her day?"

"I doubt it." Joe was drunker than I realized at first and not nearly as funny as he thought he was.

He leaned on his cane and chewed his lip. "Oops," he said, "this is your girl, huh? I knew it. Even when she was coming on to me over there, I knew it."

I looked around, hoping she didn't hear. "Not my girlfriend, Joe. Good lord, she's married. Go have a seat and be cool. I'll bring your pizza."

Joe laughed, pushed away from the counter, and turned back to his buddies. He was trying to swagger and not limp, but I could tell he still needed the cane, and walking without it was making him hurt. He circled back to the pickup window and leaned in close. "Yeah, but you wish she was your girl. I can see that in your eyes, Humpy. It's all over your face like blueberry jam." Did he have to call me Humpy?

He turned and called over his shoulder, "Hey, Frank!" The burly guy in the fatigue jacket got up and walked toward us.

"Frank, ol' buddy." Joe put his arm around the man's shoulder. "This is my little brother, Humpy."

"Sam," I inserted. I reached through the window to shake his hand. He put up a left hand, so we did an awkward shake.

"Sorry," he slurred. "This right ain't much good for now." He lifted his right arm partway up and winced when he did.

I nodded.

"This is the guy I was telling you about, the rat killer." Joe laughed. "We was in the shit together. Deep shit."

Frank shook his head. "Your brother is the man, Sam. The man."

Julie came out of the kitchen and the other customers left with a wave at the waitress. "Ah, look at her! There she is," sang Joe. "Hey, sweetheart! We were missing you."

I saw her stiffen and clench a fist. "Oh yeah?" Julie's voice was flat and indifferent. She turned away to clear the tables and tote the dishes to the kitchen. I wanted the pizza to be done. I was tempted to check it, but I knew that would make it take longer.

I had to do something, but the guys weren't really causing trouble, just being assholes. I wanted to call them out for it, Joe especially, but I just watched him walk back to his table laughing.

"What's up with you?" Julie asked, leaning into the walkway between the ovens and the pizza station and staring intently at my knotted face. "You look pissed."

"Nothin'. I got this," I said, shaking my head. "Go to the back. I'll serve 'em."

"Why? You know him?" She stood on tiptoes to peek out of the kitchen.

"Yeah, never mind. Just go. Go have a cigarette or something." Damn it, Joe.

I pulled the pizza from the oven, slid it, cut it, and boxed it. To hell if it was underdone. Then I reached in a warmer oven and pulled out the cheese bread I'd baked for me and Julie. That went into a smaller box and hit the window under the warming light. Wiping my hands on my apron, I banged out through the batwing doors into the dining room with the two boxes, marched across the room, and set them on the table.

Phelps looked straight at me across the table. "What the hell?" he said. "What's with the takeout boxes? We're eating *here*."

"No, you're not. Right, Joe?" I played a card I wasn't sure I had. I wanted these drunks outa here, not just away from Julie but away from me too. "And I threw in some cheese bread for your trouble. We're closing." I didn't risk looking at Joe. But I could feel his stare.

"You ain't throwin' us out, are ya?" Phelps said, his eyes glazed with booze. "I want to eat here with that foxy waitress." He laughed then added, "Come on, man, get us some plates."

I could feel Joe at my shoulder then his hand on my back. "Let's go, ladies," he said. "We got things to do. Phelps. Shut up and grab the pizza. Keep it flat. I don't want the cheese slidin'." The other guys laughed, and one punched Phelps in the shoulder. Joe's shoulder struck me as he passed and moved toward the door. He stretched tall and showed almost no limp. Frank grinned and lifted his chin in recognition.

"What the . . ." Phelps stuttered, halfway to his feet. His two companions laughed. He glared at me, then slowly followed Joe.

Joe turned at the door. "Are you coming, Phelps?" He was looking at me when he spoke, and he finished with a little grin just for me. "Later, little brother." He stood in the doorway for a second. "Give your girlfriend a kiss, Humpy, and tell her it's from me."

I watched the car pull away and stood for a time at the door as if I was afraid they might come back. My hands trembled, and I wiped them on my apron. It had been a small incident, just four tipsy guys getting carried away on a Friday night, but to me, it seemed more dangerous than that. I could handle being mad, but I'd never been afraid of my brother before, even when we fought. I felt like puking. The clock showed it was a few minutes before closing time, but I walked over and locked the door and then turned to sign to *CLOSED*.

In the kitchen, Julie was leaning on the counter looking out the pickup window. "That was your brother?" She came and put her arms around my torso. I froze, both surprised and excited. Suddenly I knew how an injured bird feels when someone picks it up and cradles it in one hand. Julie was warm and smelled of pizza sauce and garlic bread in a way that made me never want to smell anything else. I could feel her breasts against my ribs. I wondered which of our hearts I felt pounding. "You are such a sweetheart! Thanks for doing that," she said.

"No sweat." It was all I could say. Even that kinda stuck in my throat. I stood there frozen in her grasp.

"I mean, I can handle guys like that," she said, stepping away and untying her apron with shaking hands, "but it was nice that I didn't have to." Her eyes were full of me for the moment, something I'd never felt before, and we stood there silent with the hum of the kitchen fan in the background. I knew then she was the perfect girl for me, and the fact that she was nineteen years old, married, and the boss's daughter didn't seem to matter one damn bit.

THIRTEEN

A bird woke me with a call that sounded like a phone ringing in the woods. A varied thrush, I think, a sound of summer. I walked down the hall to take a leak and found Joe on his knees in the bathroom.

"What the hell, Joe? Use the toilet." A cold chill washed over me, and I thought he was puking in the trash can. But he lifted his head and grinned. That's when I realized he was working on the sink.

"Hey, Humpy. Finally decide to join the living? Mom's bobby pins and hair are clogging the sink drain again."

"Whatever. Clear out. I gotta take a piss."

He laid a chrome pipe elbow in the sink and gestured with a pipe wrench as he left. "Okay, but don't use the sink. It'll drain out on the floor."

I shut the door behind him. I hadn't seen Joe since the scene at Polar Pizza three nights ago and now Joe was home safe, but I didn't feel safe at all. I felt like a dog cornered by a wolf. Polar Pizza had been my last refuge, a stronghold against life at home. Joe had broken down the door of that hideaway and walked in with his bravado and boorish friends. The one place that was mine, he had soured like he had my bedroom. Now every night at my work station in front of the pizza ovens, I'd look up and worry that he would come stumbling back in the door.

And here he was again, returning from one of his drunken outings and trying to act normal, playing the handyman, the man of the house, working hard to be like Dad. As usual, Mom was all open arms and hail-fellow-well-met. Joe was full of stories and jokes until the night terrors and liquor and temper and restlessness took over, and then he was tense and mean and then gone. He stayed around for a couple of days this time, and we never talked about that night at Polar Pizza. Maybe he didn't remember or care. And yeah, I guess I was scared to bring it up.

It wasn't long before Joe disappeared again, but this time we didn't hear from him for a whole month. Mom was in a knot. Then, instead of crawling home hungover and hungry, we got a postcard saying he was well and had a job. Mom was skeptical, but the next week a letter came with a check for her to put away for him. After that, he wrote every week with a check or money order, so Mom quit worrying about one son and turned on the other.

She started on my long hair and my squabbling with Joe. "You set him off, you know. With that long hair and your attitude, not respecting what your brother's been through." We were doing yard work, raking up trash and leaves left over from winter. It was short-sleeve weather, the warmest day of June. Mom leaned on her rake and brushed her hair back from her face.

"Nobody made him go," I said. "He joined the Marines on his own. I think the war is stupid, and I am allowed to think that. I just told him so."

"Samuel Barger! Don't you dare get on your high horse! Your brother went off to fight for his country, and you should be proud of him. And you know he's paying a hard price for that."

I grabbed the loaded wheelbarrow and started for the compost pile in the backyard, but I stopped when she said, "We called it battle fatigue in the last war. Most people didn't talk about it then."

"You mean the nightmares and all that? I know. I'm not stupid."

"More than that. It changed him. He was too young," she said. "Too young to march, and too young to do the dirty work of politicians anyway." That's all she said in front of me, but I saw a lot more. Mom had never talked this way before, hinting that maybe she didn't like the war either. Like she didn't really buy all this "my country, right or wrong" crap.

"I am proud of him," I said. "We just don't agree about what he's fighting for. It's not his fault, but it's also not my fault that he doesn't like my long hair and my music and my attitude. I wasn't the one who shot him."

I headed for the backyard with the wheelbarrow and dumped the rakings against the back fence. I was mad. Mad about Joe not being the brother I wanted. Mad that my own mother wouldn't take my side, even if she might actually agree with me. Mad that I could do nothing about anything. Oh, I could cut my hair and make them happy. I'd have to cut it soon for school anyway. Why was that such a big deal, how long someone's hair was?

I was mad enough that it seemed like a good time to tackle the starter on the truck. I'd be pissed off anyway by the time I was through, since I knew nothing about installing a starter and had only the handful of tools Joe left in the garage. I had the starter under my bed, and it looked like two bolts held it on and a couple of wires had to connect to the battery and engine. The truck's starter was on the bottom of the engine and hard to get to. The bolts would surely be rusted tight, and I had only a half-assed sense of what I was doing. Other than that, it would be a piece of cake.

Lying in the dirt under that truck for an hour got the wires disconnected and one bolt removed, which rolled around in the dirt trying to get lost. "Son-of-a-bitch," I growled. "Whose idea was it

I could fix this damn truck anyway." I slammed my fist against the oil pan. Joe probably would have had this done in five minutes—the *old* Joe, anyway. The second bolt was out of sight up in the blind alley between the engine and the transmission, almost out of reach on the topside of the old starter. I could feel the edges of it, but my hand kept slipping every time I tried to get a wrench on it.

"You sound just like your father, huffing an' swearing under there." Mom had taken a break from her attack on dandelions to check up on me. She had never said I reminded her of Dad; it was always Joe that made her think of him.

"Sorry. It's this darn last bolt."

"Never mind. I've heard men work on cars before. It brings out the worst in all of you."

"Thanks. While you're here, can you see my hand?" I asked. She leaned into the mouth of the open hood. "That bolt I'm touching is what I'm trying to reach."

"Yes, I can see it. I bet you can reach it from out here."

I scrambled out of the gravel and saw she was right. I reached into the engine compartment from above and in a couple of minutes, the old starter fell out on the ground and I danced a little jig around the truck. The replacement was more cooperative, and I was soon cleaning my hands with the job all done.

Mom looked up from her dandelion war and smiled. "Well, since you're in such a good mood, come on over here and empty my wheelbarrow." She had been digging dandelions out of the lawn for nearly an hour and had filled it to the top.

I jumped on the opportunity to ask the question that I hadn't asked earlier. "So how do you really feel about the war, Mom? Are you actually okay with us fighting over there? In Vietnam, I mean."

She was still on her knees in her garden gloves and with a dandelion fork in her hand. Garden work was the only time she wore pants, and she dug in her pocket for a handkerchief and blew her nose. With a shake of her head, she said, "Sam, a mother never wants war. That's a man's thing. Mothers are the ones who lose the most. You ought to know that. But there are times . . ." Her voice trailed off and she went back to her digging.

"Yeah, but how is this our fight? It looks to me like a lot of these problems are the fault of us meddling anyway. Vietnam was a colony, Mom. They were fighting the French back in the Fifties."

"Oh Lord, Sam, those people have been fighting for thousands of years, and this is just another iteration of that. But the President said we need to be there—I certainly don't want the Communists getting their hooks in them—and, right or wrong, we need to follow our president. All this marching and protesting is just silly. Now get on that wheelbarrow and dump this crap out behind the fence on the compost pile."

I threw the last of the weeds she'd pulled into the barrow and headed for the back fence. I had guessed right about Mom, kind of reading between the lines. She didn't think I was very wrong, but she couldn't imagine breaking the rules. Of course, it was "those people," and they did look a lot like the Japanese who had tried to kill Dad during World War II. Joe, on the other hand, thought he was there to kill the "Communist gooks," and for him it didn't go much deeper than that. I could understand Mom's attitude, but Joe was a different story.

FOURTEEN

Dear Iris,

How's the fishing guide business? Life hasn't changed much since you left. I'm still the best pizza man in town and all the girls are in love with me—you better hurry back. Haha. I still don't have the pickup running yet, but I've been working on it. I bet she'll be running like a charm when you get home.

I don't know how much news you're getting, but old LBJ finally started some peace talks with the North Vietnamese. At least it's a start.

My sister came to visit. She and Mom get along fine now. When Mary first got married, I didn't think they'd ever speak to each other again. Mom wanted her to wait, but Mary wouldn't listen and marched down to City Hall the next day. Now with the baby coming, Mom's going into grandmother mode and all is forgiven.

Me and Joe fought most of the time until he disappeared. Mom was pretty worried, but we finally heard from him. He's doing okay. He even found a job. Maybe Joe and I can start some peace talks of our own when he gets back. He wants to go moose hunting this fall. We'll see.

Just your friend,
Sam

My summer was a time of separation. David was off in Fairbanks then fish camp. Iris was working for her father off on some river, and Joe was gone God knows where. It was just me and Mom, working and eating and sleeping. I went hiking in the mountains when I could and made great plans for a trip to the cabin back home on the bluff. I cooked pizza and hot sandwiches with a passion, and I also realized that Julie was just a fantasy for me, something I cooked up in the kitchen with the smell of marinara sauce and garlic. She treated me like a man, not a boy, and that turned my head for a while. But I figured out that was all there was to it.

Each week, I poured my criticism of the imperfect world out in a letter to Iris. I reported news of the war and the protests against it. I told her stories about my hikes in the woods and the books I'd read like *Black Like Me* and *The Naked Ape,* books that made me think about a new world full of ideas. I never wrote many letters before, except to Gramma and Grampa back in Ohio for Christmas and after my birthday thanking them for a gift. The act of writing to Iris made me feel closer to her though, and I started counting the days until she would be back.

Hey Iris, what's happening?
Well, here I am again, pen in hand, and my brain is empty. Not much going on except the Fourth of July passed without any fireworks at the Barger Ranch. With Joe gone, me and Mom are getting along good. She's not so worried about Joe since he's not stumbling in drunk every couple of days. She worries more about Mrs. Kennedy who now

has buried three sons. Moms worry about other moms, I guess.

I went for a hike the other day when I got lonesome for you. I hitchhiked out the highway and prowled the hillside trails along Turnagain Arm. I was tempted to stay on the highway and go all the way home to the cabin on the bluff, but this was better than nothing. I sure miss that place. Maybe I'll take you there someday—if you're nice. Haha. It was a good weather day, and I could look north to the Alaska Range and see Denali and Foraker, and Redoubt Volcano. I wanted to go into that wild country, like where you are. When I climbed up a ways there weren't no people, and it all felt pretty wild even though Anchorage was just around the corner.

I saw a moose on the way down, and that got me thinking about hunting and how I'd like to be hunting for bull moose with Joe and maybe forgetting the unhappy crap we been through. Even that thought made me sad though, so I tried to think of happy things, like you and me together again. You're probably thinking, "Oh Sam, going all macho with this hunting thing," but it's not like that. It's like a family tradition and a way to remember my dad. I have been reading The Naked Ape, *and Desmond Morris says that hunting helped make humans smarter and more cooperative as we evolved. It's in our genes. And it might be the only thing Joe and I have in common anymore.*

Just your friend,
Sam

Two weeks after I mailed my first letter, I got a postcard from Iris. All summer she only wrote postcards, but that was enough to keep me writing. That first postcard was a photo of a grizzly bear standing in a stream with a salmon in his mouth. She had written across the photo *Catch and Repeat.*

Sam,
I just finished a good cry over Robert Kennedy. I feel so hopeless about the future.

Keep writing,
Iris

Each postcard was a gift I waited for day after day, and when it came I soared for a time, feeling that I had won her at last. And then days would pass, then a week, then two weeks, until my hope would fade. I would imagine her taking up with some clever fly fisherman or the son of some rich businessman on vacation. Then when I'd be at the end of hope, that's when another card would come.

Sam,
I don't get the whole hunting thing, but I don't hate you for it. Labor Day March for Peace! Let's do it.

Power to the people,
Iris

This postcard had a photo of a bull moose standing in a pond. Iris wrote across the top, *Make meat, not War!*

Iris's postcards were few and far in between, but they kept me writing, so I wrote letters each week, usually late at night after a day working the pizza parlor. The midnight sun made me want to stay up all night and use every minute of the summer that I wanted to come to an end, because at its end Iris would come home. I signed each letter, *Just your friend, Sam.*

Of course, the end of summer might also bring Joe home, and I wasn't ready to go through that again.

Sam,
How's the pizza business? Have you taken over the place yet? Don't plan anything for Labor Day. The March for Peace is at

Delaney Park that day. We could go together. This is our chance to be part of something bigger. Guess what! I miss you.

Iris

A postcard of a Dall sheep with great rolling horns posing on a rock. Iris's caption read, *Sam the Ram,* with an arrow pointing at the horns.

Iris,

I'm glad you'll be back for the peace march. There is so little being done here to speak against the war, except Senator Gruening. He makes me proud to be an Alaskan. The other politicians have sold out, I think, but we can't stop marching or we will be invisible. Someday maybe Joe will understand. I think even my mom is changing her attitude, but she won't admit it to me. She's sick of watching news reports of more dead young soldiers. I'm so glad we won't have LBJ in the White House next year. Maybe that will change things.

Guess what? I got my driver's license. About time, huh? Well, Joe was right about one thing. And the test wasn't that hard since I've been driving a lot without a license—don't tell anyone. I had plenty of practice with the parking part. It was hard to remember all those laws for the written test, but the rest was easy. It was worth the two-hour wait at the motor vehicle department or whatever it's called. And, you guessed it, I got the pickup put back together. I took off the old fender and hood, all by myself. Applause, please. I got parts at the junkyard that I also installed. Impressed? You should be. All have to do is get the old girl running and I'll be set. You might even get a ride in it if you're nice to me.

I finished the book Black Like Me *and it made me think about how superficial we are as people. I can't imagine the experiences that man Griffin had visiting the South, pretending to be a Black man. I wonder if I would ever have that kind of courage. Maybe on Labor Day we'll find out. Lots of people are down on the protesters, calling us commies and traitors and cowards. We know better.*

I miss your freckles.

Just your friend,
Sam

FIFTEEN

We were five minutes from closing time and I was mopping the dining room when Iris walked into Polar Pizza in a golden tan, cut-off jeans, and a braless white T-shirt. She said, "Hey," and I was sure glad I wrote her those letters. The summer sun had given her a million freckles and I wanted to count each one.

"Hey." I leaned on my mop and looked at her eyes, her hair, her brown smooth legs, her breasts, her smile, the freckles, her breasts. Then I said what any guy would say in that situation. "You want some pizza?"

"Sure."

"Good. There's one in the oven."

She sat at a table by the door while I mopped around her. "How you been?"

I held up my mop. "Oh, I'm cleaning up in the pizza business. Makin' lots of dough."

We laughed together. Then we left together in her dad's station wagon with the pizza in a box. We drove to Goose Lake and ate pizza sitting on the moss under a birch tree, then walked through the woods along the shore. Iris talked. I listened. She talked about her work and her dad and her parents' divorce as if she hadn't talked to anyone all summer. It was like she had saved it all up to share with me. "You wrote me," she said. "I didn't think you would."

"I told you I would."

She leaned toward me like she does when she's about to say something really serious. "I know, and you kept writing."

"Yup, I did."

"But you weren't supposed to. It was just supposed to be a line, something you say, like 'see ya later.' But you did, and that was so sweet."

"And you sent postcards," I said. I pointed to a loon cruising the waters of the lake. An eagle flew over and the loon began to call a loud, cackling alarm. "Hear the loon?" I said.

"So wild and strange," she said. "I love it." She sat under a tree and reached a hand to me. I thought what a perfect wild setting it was, and flopped down beside her in moss soft as a mattress.

"Sorry I flunked letter writing though," she said. "The cards were the best I could do."

"No, you didn't flunk. I thought they were great. So I remind you of a Dall sheep, huh?"

"Maybe. And . . . Well, I was so impressed that you wrote every week that I brought you a present." From her pocket she drew a shiny peace symbol on a chain and held it up.

"Wow, that's nice. But I didn't get you anything."

"Come on. You wrote like twenty letters. I didn't write many postcards," she said. "And you wrote great letters. Maybe we're even." She leaned in and put it around my neck. Then she kissed me, a soft, lingering kiss on the lips.

"Welcome home," I said.

I took her arm and pulled her to me, and kissed her. I kissed her chatty mouth, her freckled cheeks, her hair that smelled of herbal shampoo. Then I put my arms around her and kept kissing her. At first, she got stiff and hesitant, then I felt the weight of her against my arm and her mouth relax and she was kissing me back. It was the kiss I had been waiting for all summer, and I didn't want it to end, so we stayed locked there together until she finally pulled away and said, "What was that?"

"I'm tired of just hanging out," I said. I kissed her again, and she put her arms around my neck.

"Shut up and kiss me," she said. So I did.

"Something's come between us." I grabbed a stick that jutted up from the moss and tossed it over my shoulder. She laughed and lay back on the grass. I could taste the pizza on her mouth and the sweat on her neck. And then we were making out without talking. Her hand went inside my shirt on my back, then in my hair. I found her breast under her T-shirt, and it fit in my hand like a ball of pizza dough but firmer and warmer. She didn't pull my hand away, and we entered a place where time stood still.

I slid my hand down her belly and along her thigh. She moaned and bit my ear when I found the warm spot between her legs. "Leave the buttons alone," she said and bit my ear again. I laughed, a loud laugh that rattled in the trees above us.

"What?" She pushed me up and locked on my eyes. "You laughing at me?"

I kissed her lightly, my hand still between her legs. "Desmond Morris," I chuckled again. I couldn't help it. "He was right."

"Oh good. About what?" She pulled my hand away and held it, lacing our fingers.

"The earlobes. He said earlobes were erogenous zones, like your breasts and other parts. I was just thinking, wow, he's right. I don't know why but it made me laugh."

"Oh." I covered her mouth with mine before she could say more. Then she turned her head and I nibbled her tiny earlobe. We stopped talking for a minute or an hour—I couldn't tell—until she whispered in my ear, "I gotta go, Sam," gently pushing me up and away.

"Yeah," I admitted, "I'll catch hell if I'm home late. Lucky for me, my mom sleeps pretty soundly."

"Yeah, well, my mom sleeps like a guard dog, up at every sound. No getting past her," Iris laughed as she stood up and pulled her shirt down. "You are pretty good with your hands there, pizza man." She brushed the bits of moss and crushed leaves away. I blushed and turned away.

"I do my best."

She punched me. "You're a bad boy, but this was fun," she said, her hand on my back. "I like hanging out with you."

I thought we were doing more than hanging out, but I just said, "Me too."

Iris drove me home, and we spent five minutes kissing goodbye. Just as I was getting out of the car, she said, "Oh yeah, we need to get ready for the Labor Day peace march. The war isn't over, you know. We're making posters tomorrow. You're gonna come, right?"

"Yeah. But I thought we were on R and R just for tonight. Even Marines get time away from the front. Let's talk about that tomorrow."

"I know. It's not fair, you know," she said, "that we get to just go through life regular while guys are over there fighting and dying for a lie. You don't want more guys to end up like your brother."

I didn't want this conversation. I didn't want to ruin this perfect night, but it was there and she'd opened her mouth and it was like Pandora releasing all the bad things that I had kept penned in. I had to answer, to say something. "Isn't that what the politicians say they're fighting for? You know. To keep us free. For all of this!" I swept my arms around like I was presenting the whole neighborhood on stage. "I don't want to talk or think about Joe or his damn war, not tonight."

And I walked away. I walked across the street to my house. I walked away from the war, from the protest marches, and Joe and everything for this one evening. I was going to let Sam Barger have his moment. I wanted to savor it like a great piece of pie, experiencing both the moment and the time after the moment. Tomorrow I would let the world back in.

She called the next day. "Hey, smartass. That was quite the exit last night."

The phone was cold against my ear and I could hear her breathing, wanting to say more but biting her tongue. "I'm sorry," I said. "It's . . . It's just that I wanted that moment, that time. Just us without the outside pushing in."

"Okay, fine." Her voice went businesslike. "So you don't want to help me? I could use some help, you know. I promised people."

"Sure. I told you, I'm in." I could tell we were talking past each other, maybe because she didn't want to talk about us. "We're making posters, right?"

"Yeah, the day before, but tonight we are having a planning meeting. Can you come? I know you have work and all that."

"Sure." As usual, I couldn't say no. And I didn't want to. As Iris said, this was a chance to be part of something bigger. I had my moment, and now I was back open for business. My love life had to wait.

About a dozen people were at the meeting, with Iris and me as the only high school kids. The leaders were serious and intense, planning the march like it was military raid of some sort, and they talked about how the cops or pro-war people might try to stop us from marching. It got me wound up so that when I was watching the news later, everything felt more real and closer now. I couldn't help but see myself in the lines of marchers, shoulder to shoulder in the street, chanting and waving signs, and then when the police came with helmets and shields and batons. I was part of this now. This weekend I would be on the street taking a stand.

SIXTEEN

"What's wrong?" David asked. "You out of gas?"

"No. The gauge reads half a tank. It's probably something in the ignition."

David was home from Fairbanks, and we were trying to start the '57. We'd been cranking off and on for thirty minutes with little breaks to fiddle with the carburetor and wiggle the spark plug wires like we knew what were doing.

"Crap!" I shut the hood. "This damn truck hasn't run in over a year. I guess I can't expect it to fire right up. Let's try some starter fluid. Look under the seat and in the glove box for some. I should have known my plan wouldn't work."

"What plan?" David asked with his head under the seat.

"No big deal. I was going to take us cruisin'. I got my license, and I thought we could drive over, pick up Iris, and make some signs for the march." I spoke like I was relaxed and offhand about the whole thing.

"If you get this rig running," he said, "you need to pick up Iris and go get laid. You don't need me for that." He crawled out of the truck with a can in his hand. "Well, here's the starter fluid. Let's give it one more chance."

"You do have good ideas, but I don't think we're there yet. I haven't made it to home plate yet, but I haven't struck out either. Now go take off the air cleaner and spray that go juice into the carburetor when I crank the engine."

David looked under the hood. "Where's the air cleaner?" I scrambled out and showed him the wing nut that attached the air cleaner to the carburetor, then climbed back in to turn the key. The engine cranked, fired, and died. We tried several times before I called it quits.

"You got your license?" David replaced the air cleaner and picked up the last of the tools we were using and tossed them in the toolbox. "I thought your mom nixed that."

"Well, it's like Joe said. You don't need your mom's permission to get a driver's license. I just took my learner's permit down to the DMV and took the test. She doesn't even know. Come on. I brought home pizza last night."

We headed for the house with David shaking his head. "I don't want to be around when you tell her."

"Me either. Anyway, I thought I'd tell her when Joe gets home and she's all happy again." We sprawled on the couch and watched a game show while devouring a mushroom and sausage pizza. I told him the rest of the plan. "I wanted to get the truck running for Joe, kind of a peace offering. Now it'll just be one more thing to piss him off. That and the peace march."

"Nah, he's a pretty good mechanic, right? The truck will be nothing. He'll just go all big brother on ya and have it running in fifteen minutes. Then he'll give you shit about being a dipshit."

I pushed the last piece of pizza his way and chuckled. "I love your optimism."

David shook his head, "Not at all. When he hears about you at the peace protest, he'll kick a lake in your ass and stomp it dry. He ain't going to like that target you're wearing around your neck either."

I felt the peace symbol with my fingers and held it up. "A gift from Iris. Yeah, Joe probably won't like that, but tough. You're coming with me, right?"

"To your ass kicking? No thanks, I'll pass."

"No, stupid, to the peace march."

"Yeah. No. Maybe." David wiped pizza sauce off the vinyl tablecloth and looked thoughtful. "So you and Joe haven't made peace yet, I take it." He pulled a pack of cigarettes from his pocket and shook the pack so several slid out so he could grab one with his teeth. It was the kind of slick, right-out-the-movies gesture David was good at. He looked up at me as if he couldn't light up his smoke until he heard the answer.

"Shit. It's all screwed up," I said. "Before he left, it was like Joe kept reliving the battles in his sleep, but when he was awake he just talked about silly stuff like throwing cans of C-rations at the Vietnamese, and them throwing back the lima beans and ham. Stupid, huh?"

David finally lit his cigarette. "You and your brother are fighting over lima beans?"

"Like I said, it's stupid. See, Joe says the GIs don't like the lima beans and ham, so that's what they usually throw to the people begging for food. But it turns out the Vietnamese hate limas just as much as the GIs. It's a stupid story, but that's the idea. He would talk about stuff like that. And then when he tried to sleep, he'd have nightmares, screaming and yelling like he's back in it. And trust me, those dreams ain't about lima beans. I mean, he's been 'in the shit,' as he calls it, but he won't talk about it. Instead, it's all about their stupid-ass pranks and the whores in Saigon."

"That's some heavy shit, man."

"Yeah, tell me about it. I finally wised up and don't talk about how wrong the war is. In fact, I didn't talk about anything.

And he's been gone most of the summer, but he wrote Mom and said he's coming home so maybe things will be different."

"Man, family fights are a bitch, especially long ones." He stubbed out the cigarette in Mom's ashtray and brushed some ashes off his corduroy bell-bottoms. "That's why I like Gramps. No matter what it is, he doesn't make a fight out of it. He just lets you talk, and he listens. There ain't no fights that way, no words to get in the way. You two need to get back to the woods. That's what Gramps would say. 'Go to hunting camp.'"

"Yeah, well, maybe. Me and Joe are talking about going moose hunting, but I don't know." I walked out to the backyard and looked at the truck with its three-color paint job. I looked at the mountains in the distance with the forest on their shoulders. I wanted to be there. It was so close, there was no reason not to.

"Maybe you should come with us," I said. "Show us the Athabascan way."

David snickered. "I never shot nothin' before."

I felt the words more than heard them, and I gawked at the courage it took for him to call himself down like that. His words hung in the air. Here was an Alaska Native, supposedly born as part of the land, but he had grown up in the cities of Fairbanks and Anchorage.

"Yup, that's me," he said. "Never hunted, never fished, and sure never spent the night in the woods. Hell, I only know the Anchorbascan way."

"Anchorbascan?" I asked.

David laughed. "Yeah. That's what Gramps calls us Athabascan Indians who live in the big city instead of the village. Get it? Anchorage, Anchorbascans."

I laughed and shook my head. "Damn, David. You're a case."

"You're right. You'd think a half-breed Athabascan would improve your chances. Not this Indian. I spent all summer at fish camp proving to the whole family that I am not a Bush Native. They couldn't get rid of me fast enough. I am a hunter, but not a moose hunter. I'm a hunter for love!"

"How could you not want to go moose hunting? Guns, no school, no parents."

"No shower, no TV, no women!" David said. "No thanks." He looked at the clock. "Got to go, man."

David walked out to the sidewalk and down to the boulevard to catch the city bus home. I couldn't stop thinking about what he had said. *Go to hunting camp.*

When Dad was alive, when the old Joe was with us, they would be getting ready for hunting now, cleaning rifles and telling hunting stories at the dinner table. He and Joe would start scouting for moose in the woods around the cabin, and sometimes I'd tag along.

I used to be Joe's shadow then, following him into the woods whenever he would let me. I remembered sitting by a pond during a moose-scouting trip and catching a movement across the water. I'd froze, like Joe taught me, letting only my eye move to scan to shadowed woods. Joe had pointed as a coyote stepped out of the shadows into an open spot along the shore, its dog face turned toward us, curious and cautious. Then it spun and disappeared into the black shelter of the forests. The coyotes seemed to live on the edge of human places like they wanted to be close, but were scared to be too close.

Twice I saw coyotes that way, and when we still lived on the bluff I would hear them at night through my open window. The coyote's call was more of a yelping chatter and was different from the sharp howl of the neighbor's sled dogs and even the spooky howl of the wolf, which I had heard just once in the deepest part of winter. Joe had said coyotes sometimes called when they were separated from the pack and trying to find their way home.

Maybe in Joe's crazy, jarhead way he was like a lone coyote. Maybe like David said, it was up to me to find a way to be brothers again. Hunting was one thing that sounded good to Joe, and something I wanted too. We didn't have Dad, but we had his hunting way. I started formulating a plan, a plan that had Joe and me in the woods, just the two of us on a moose hunt.

SEVENTEEN

"Come to the march, David. There'll be chicks. They love this kind of stuff." I had called him twice to talk him into being my wingman. It took the promise of food and women, but finally I lured David Nelson to join the Labor Day March for Peace. I even got him to come to a church basement the day before for planning and sign painting. He showed up in bell-bottom cords, harness boots, and a paisley shirt.

"Going on *The Dating Game*?" I asked. He looked at my dirty jeans and shook his head in disappointment.

I introduced him to the main organizer, some college kid named Garrett with curly hair and a tie-dye shirt. "Excellent," Garrett said. "May I ask, David, are you Alaska Native?" David nodded his reply as he looked past the guy at the three braless college girls handing out poster-making materials and sexy smiles. "We are proud to have your people join this effort. The voice of Alaska Natives is critical to the movement." He grinned like a car salesman and wouldn't stop shaking David's hand.

"No sweat," David said. "Maybe I should help with the poster paper." He pulled his hand free and moved off to make himself invaluable to the coeds in cutoffs.

All day long, he got lots of attention for being Alaska Native, and he let the college girls take him in hand and set him up with a sign that read, *True Alaskans for Peace.* My sign said, *Peace Now!* I was jealous of the Vietnam vet with sideburns and a mustache who had a sign that read, *Make Love, not War.*

Iris was all business when we made posters, but when we went to the kitchen to clean the big coffee percolator, she hugged me from behind and pinched my earlobe. I reached back and swatted her ass. "You little devil," I said. She giggled and kissed me. Then Garrett started his speech and shattered our moment.

"You all have seen the news," he said. "You know what to expect. The pigs are just waiting for an excuse to shut us down, but if we follow the law and hold a peace march they have no recourse. They can't interfere. We are in the right, and we are not alone." I looked around the room at the eager faces. I expected more like a big mob of people instead of two dozen. Garrett must have expected a crowd too because he talked like he was addressing a thousand of us.

"We have to be ready," Garrett continued. "We have to be ready to be harassed and attacked, even arrested." He was pacing now as the nervous energy was building in him. "But this is important enough that these things don't matter. We have to show that Alaska has a voice too, that Alaskans stand against the war too. In Chicago this summer, the voices of the young people were shut out of the Democratic convention. *Democratic*, now that's an ironic name." We all clapped as we remembered the violence that erupted in Chicago. I remembered the news footage of cops beating college students marching outside the convention hall. People had died in the streets during what was supposed to be a peaceful protest.

"This kind of violence won't happen if we stay on our designed route and don't become violent ourselves," Garrett insisted. "But we have to be ready. Don't fool yourselves. There are people who don't want us to be heard. They don't want us to act." He raised his voice now, and I wondered if he had practiced this. "We will march, we will be heard. We will overcome!"

We all clapped and cheered, our voices ringing hollow in the church basement where we were gathered. I hugged Iris and kissed her, admiring the fire in her eyes. I felt my heart racing. Tomorrow we would make a difference.

The March started at the east end of Delaney Park in an empty parking lot with a cool fall breeze flapping our signs. I counted thirty-five people when we started, but Iris said she knew it would grow. We were with a mixed bunch of college students, passionate religious folks, and even some Vietnam vets who we all honored with a special reverence because they had been there and came back to take a stand.

The weather was warm, but I wore a heavy coat, the only armor I had against attackers with billy clubs or baseball bats. I'd at least have a little padding if we fell or were dragged in handcuffs to some police van. I'd maybe lose less skin. I was even wearing leather gloves, just in case, but for tear gas we had no protection.

"Remember," said some guy with long hair and round, John Lennon glasses, "we may be attacked by the pigs, or by our enemies, people who hate what we stand for. But we must stand for nonviolence. Do not fight back! We must be the peace we ask for! We'll raise our voices but not our fists!"

We clapped and cheered, and three more people trotted up to join us. "Peace Now! Peace Now!" The chanting made me proud of my sign, and I shook it to the rhythm of the chant as we started our march. I was anxious but confident. Trouble was coming, but we would stay strong.

Delaney Park was once an airfield so it's long and narrow, running east and west for about twelve blocks through downtown Anchorage. Some of the park was ball fields, but much of it was open grass. We marched three or four abreast, carrying our signs like rifles on our shoulders or pumping them up and down above our heads. As we moved along the north side of the park, nothing happened. Absolutely nothing. Cars passed and people stared, some waved, a few honked, and one or two flipped the bird, but no one attacked, and no cops showed up.

We reached the end of the park completely safe. We handed out flyers to people who walked by or rolled down their car windows and invited them to join us. We stopped under the giant spruce flagpole where two guys played guitars, and we sang songs by Joan Baez and Bob Dylan. Someone handed out mimeograph song sheets and we sang "Universal Soldier." That made me remember the day I decided I was ready to stand up for what I believed, even if it brought more trouble than I wanted. As we sang, Iris held my hand and leaned on my arm. I felt powerful, important, alive. Her voice was clean and fresh like spring water, and we swayed to the music, captured by the moment.

We marched again, moving across the west end of the park where some hippies playing frisbee quit their game and joined us. We marched past kids playing catch and a guy playing fetch with his dog. By the time we looped back around toward our starting point, I figured we were nearly fifty strong, and the fervor rose in the group. Still, no one came to confront us. The sun brought heat, and I was sweating in the heavy coat and gloves. When we saw a police patrol car roll by slowly, looking us over, we waved our placards and chanted louder.

"It's the pigs!" someone yelled. The cops didn't seem to hear and drove on by. Three guys pulled out a lighter and burned their draft cards, waving the burning papers high in the air. I wished I had one so I could join them. No cars even slowed down. A couple of drivers honked their horns, but otherwise, we had no audience at all.

I started to feel strangely disappointed, invisible even, and my energy waned. It was like no one cared one way or another. I had come ready for a confrontation, cops marching shoulder to shoulder to drive back the surge of our impassioned throng. I wanted us to flood into the streets and stop traffic, to surge like a bore tide down this back street to Fifth Avenue where we couldn't be ignored. But we seemed like we were just a group of people walking through the park carrying signs.

A cop pulled up when we were disbanding and rolled down his cruiser window. "Pick up your trash if you would, folks," he said. "Leave the park as you found it. And take your signs with you."

And then it was over. Without lines of cops with billy clubs, without mad vigilantes charging out of the crowd with bats and fists to batter us to the pavement, it was over without a flood of passion down the city streets of Anchorage. At Kent State, the National Guard killed students who were protesting. At Berkeley they had a pitched battle between the police and protesters. On college campuses across the US, tear gas and billy clubs were the order of the day, and we got none of that. One young newspaper reporter with a camera was all the attention we got.

We were just a bunch of long-haired people walking in winter coats on a cloudy day in September, carrying signs about peace. And I was dismayed. I wanted drama, a fist-in-your-face confrontation, and all I got was a walk in the park. I took the sign I'd carried and marched to the corner of the Delaney Park lawn and drove my survey stake into the ground so that every car that passed would read, *Peace Now!* I didn't see the newspaper reporter with his camera pointed at me clicking away.

EIGHTEEN

Pete was drinking coffee with his feet on a chair, reading the evening paper, while a fresh pot of pizza sauce simmered in the kitchen. "Well, hotshot," he growled, looking at me over the sports page, "you certainly stepped in it this time."

"What? Did I leave the pizza oven on or the fridge door open?" Pete had never chewed my ass in all the months I'd been there. I'd never seen him angry or raise his voice at anyone before. I figured I messed up somehow because Pete was looking disgusted as hell.

"Don't you read the paper, Sam? Your little protest march has made you the talk of the town."

Well, that didn't make any sense to me because I had seen the morning paper. All it said about the Labor Day peace march was one paragraph in the City News section under the headline "Peace March a Labor of Futility." The one-paragraph story said: *A spirited band of sign-carrying marchers failed to draw much attention and quickly disbanded after parading the length of the Delaney Park.* Yes, I read it enough times that I memorized that line.

"Gee, what's your beef, Pete? You're the first person to mention it. It wasn't any big deal, pretty much a flop." I started for the kitchen still shaking my head, wondering what had him all steamed up.

"Well, if I had my picture on the front page of the newspaper it would be a big deal to me."

That stopped me dead in my tracks, and I turned to look at him. He was holding the evening newspaper up for me to see, and there on the bottom of the front page was a picture of me sticking my protest sign in the dirt of Delaney Park. I looked strangely overdressed for early September, and the wind had blown my hair up so I looked even more wild and pissed off than I actually was at the time.

"Holy shit," I said. I guess most of us would think it was pretty cool to have our picture in the paper, but I felt my stomach tighten, and the room felt suddenly smaller and hotter.

Julie came up behind me and patted me on the back. "Oo-la-la! Don't you look tough," she teased. "Can I have your autograph?"

Pete wasn't amused. "You better get it before his brother breaks every bone in his body, and I wouldn't blame him. Good lord, boy. Your brother comes back from fighting and you're out there marching, saying what he did was all for nothin'?" Pete turned the newspaper around and started reading aloud. "A young protester posts an illegal sign on the Delaney Park lawn in the biggest act of civil disobedience at the Labor Day peace march on Monday. A lonely few dozen marchers went generally unnoticed when they marched in protest against the war in Vietnam."

"Wow," said Julie, "didn't know you were a hippie. Wasn't your brother wounded over there?"

"Yeah, and he could have died," said Pete. "Sounds like you drew quite a crowd, Sam, haha. What a dipshit. How you think your mom feels right now? And your brother?"

"Come on, Pete. I was just standing up for what I think." I thought about walking out right then and not giving Pete a chance to fire me.

"What you did was go against your family and your country. That's what you did."

"Oh, Dad. Leave him alone." Julie had gone back to wiping tables, but she was there to get my back, and that felt good.

"All right, all right," Pete said, folding his paper. "Just keep your politics outa my pizza parlor, Barger, or you'll be out on your ass." He picked up his coat and walked out the door with the newspaper lying on the table and my ass hanging out in the wind. I stood and watched as he stomped out to his boxy Rambler station wagon. As he backed out of his parking place, he rolled down the window and glared at me through the glass door.

I flopped down on the nearest chair. "Holy crap, I thought he was going to fire me," I said.

Julie came over and patted me on the back. "Nah, he likes you too much. He's just blowing off steam. He told me you had a lotta guts to do that, but he won't tell you that."

Just then the phone rang with a pizza order, and then customers came in. Before I knew it, I was making pizza and toasting sandwiches like it was just another day at Polar Pizza. But the knot in my stomach wouldn't go away.

Wednesday at school wasn't any better than going to work. Even people who liked me were giving me crap, and David was having a field day ribbing me. Halverson saw me in the hall and said, "Way to go with civil disobedience, Mr. Thoreau."

As if that wasn't enough, the vice principal got in my face between classes. "I can't see the ears, Mr. Barger. Can't see the ears. Get that hair cut."

It had been a battle all year between the kids and the administration about how long our hair should be. It was like they were convinced that guys with hair over their collars couldn't learn. "But the rules don't say anything about the ears. It's about the collar!" I responded.

Around us, the students surged into classrooms and corridors like a mass of sockeye salmon heading upstream. There was a rumble and a tension in the movement as bodies bumped and slid past. I felt it all closing in and I was suddenly hot, and I smelled the heat of other kids. The vice principal's spectacled face stared up at me, the chin jutted forward. I realized I had grown and now the man had to look up at me. "Don't push it with me, Mr. Barger. Don't test me!"

"Okay, okay. I'll tell the barber to do better next time."

A finger came up to poke my chest, at the peace symbol hanging outside my shirt, and I was helpless against an impulse to slap it away. But before the finger reached me, before my hand reacted, relief came. A sudden crash down the hall pushed the flow of students against us as a fight erupted just steps away. The vice principal stumbled, and then the angry little man pushed through the throng to 'Mister' some other kids. I slid into the flood of students and made myself scarce.

Iris and I were having lunch and catching up on the summer when David showed up and teased me about getting busted by the VP. "I told you I should get after those lovely locks of yours," he said.

I wasn't laughing. I hadn't cut my hair all summer and had gotten to like the feel of it falling over my collar and covering my neck. I even started tying it back in a stubby ponytail for work. At first it made me feel silly and self-conscious, but I got used to it. Now I was feeling bald without that wad of hair at the back of my neck. David already had to trim it for me just that morning to make it legal for school. Then I showed up and got busted anyway because it was still too long. I knew this hair thing was silly. Short or long, what did it matter? But it was all I had, my long hair and my picture on the front page of the paper.

Only Iris said anything nice, and even she embarrassed me by saying she cut out the newspaper photo and pinned it to her bedroom wall. But she still was kind of distant, not holding hands in the hall, and just giving me a little peck when I tried to make out with her. I liked the idea of being in her bedroom, but let's be honest, all this hoopla wouldn't have happened if it hadn't been for her. Not that I didn't believe in the peace movement, but I just wasn't usually the guy that liked to stand up and get attention, and I was getting more than I wanted.

The strangest part of that week, though, was Mom. She didn't say a word about any of it—the peace march, the photo, or how Joe would feel about it—and I sure didn't bring it up. I found the Tuesday paper in the trash and dusted off the coffee grounds so I could cut out the picture and stow it in my sock drawer.

Thursday night we watched the news and learned that 114 Marines were killed in an "operation" in a place called the Que Son Valley, but neither one of us said anything. I knew Mom was thinking how good it was that Joe was safe. I knew she was also thinking about 114 moms who weren't so lucky. One hundred fourteen was a real number, and it made me proud that I had stood up and got my picture in the paper doing it. She hadn't said anything about it to me, so I just let it ride. As much as I wanted to show her those numbers and make her see that was why I was part of the peace movement, I just let our unspoken truce in the Barger house continue.

By Friday I figured everything had blown over. Unfortunately Joe was due home Saturday, and I had no idea how he was going to react. Joe was a big wild card all on his own. Restless and out of better options, I headed to the Back to School Dance with David, who wanted to cruise the chicks. Iris was at her dad's again for the weekend, and it wouldn't have been her kind of thing anyway. I found myself holding up one side of the gymnasium wall, with the other guys without dates. We all stood watching the dancers while we stared helplessly at the clusters of girls in their own little lifeboats along the opposite walls. The girls were chatting in animated little clusters while we boys stood silent like sentries, guarding the wall with our hands in our pockets.

Out in the center of the gym, girls in short dresses and pantyhose and boys in slacks and collared shirts danced to the Beatles and Creedence Clearwater Revival, while teachers in suits and ties stood sternly on the sidelines or sorted through the stack of vinyl records for songs too sexy for a school dance. When the DJ put on the Righteous Brothers, couples moved close to hold each other for slow dancing. The vice principal walked among them, tapping a boy on the shoulder when his hands strayed to his date's butt. "I want to see some daylight between you two," he told one couple who looked like they were ready to find a backseat in a far corner of the parking lot. I realized dancing was something Iris and I hadn't done together, but watching made me miss her anyway.

The music picked up and I ventured across the expanse of polished wood to dance with a girl I had talked to a lot in last year's classes. I made silly jokes while we shook and wiggled, trying to do a combination of the twist and the jerk to pounding rock music. But the conversation couldn't hold up after the music ended, and I was back on the wall with the other guys, most of them wishing they could be shooting hoops instead. I left David trying to charm a new girl from California and wandered out into the hallway and then to the parking lot.

Two boys I knew came by. "Hey, Barger, come on! They're slugging out behind the temporaries. Blow off the dance! It's lame."

I followed them across the parking lot to three wood-frame gray buildings squatting in the gravel. They were temporary classrooms, and behind them, out of sight of the main building, was where kids went to smoke, fight, or make out. Tonight it featured all three, and even some small bottles of liquor were making the rounds. A crowd of boys blocked the view of the combat, and I had to walk through them to see.

Jacob Phelps, looking older than some of the teachers, was standing in a circle of boys with a cigarette in hand. His voice was louder and nastier than anyone else's. "What about some of you punks? Wanna slug with me?" he said, gesturing in my direction. The smaller and younger boys stood back from the rowdy talk, leaning against the wooden building and letting the bigger, manlike guys butt heads. I had grown over the last year and now stood tall among the others. The sight of Phelps had me flushed and irritated.

"What about you?" He pointed at me and I wondered if he remembered that night with Joe at the pizza parlor.

"You mean me?"

"Yeah, you. Or are you like the rest of these gutless wonders?"

I didn't hesitate. In an instant I went from timid to pissed off. I couldn't tell if Phelps recognized me or not, but it didn't matter. His sneer and cock-sure attitude were enough. "Sure. I'll slug with you."

Phelps tossed his cigarette to the ground and dragged two lines in gravel with his toe. I dropped my jacket and walked over to step on one line. We stood about eighteen inches apart. Phelps sneered and blew cigarette smoke in my face. I could smell liquor too. With us standing that close it was obvious that we were about the same height, but he had more shoulder and meat. "Ready?" he asked. I'd seen this game at parties, so I knew the rules said each guy had to stand on the line and say, *Ready*. We'd take turns slugging each other on the shoulder until one gave up or moved both feet off the line.

"Ready," I said. He punched as soon as I spoke but he had rushed his swing and didn't put full weight behind the punch. It landed high on the outside of my shoulder, and I had to move one foot off the line to keep my balance. "Ready?" I asked, quickly.

"Ready."

I smiled when I saw him lean slightly to his left with his weight on that foot. He wasn't expecting a lefty and was bracing his whole body to take a hit on the left shoulder. My left fist hit his right shoulder instead. He stumbled off the line, tripped, and fell.

"Yeah! Bring the lumber, southpaw!" yelled a tall, slender boy in a leather jacket. "You're down and out, Phelps!"

"I'm in!" yelled a burly guy from the shadows with a girl on his arm. Calvin Rafka was short and thick like a football lineman. He pulled off his wool shirt, exposing bulging biceps under his T-shirt.

"Hey, Barger," he said. "Nice picture in the paper the other day. I'll be glad to knock you off the line."

"Ready?" I asked, though my pride had faded and I felt suddenly thin and frail. Exposed.

"Ready." Calvin didn't even shift a foot when I hit him. He just stretched and shrugged to loosen his shoulder before smashing my arm with a right that felt like it was made of oak, not meat and bone.

He laughed when I staggered. "Stay up, stay up!" he said. "I want to hit you again."

I wavered but kept one foot on the line. My shoulder was pounding with pain from the two punches it had taken already, but I was feeding off a rush of excitement and strength. I shook my arm with the hand open.

"Attaboy!" called Calvin. The circle of students tightened and the voices closed around us. I could tell that he liked the challenge the game presented, two strong opponents on either side of the line. That was different from Phelps, who seemed to just want to hurt people. I felt the center of that circle lift, and I could hear the music from the gym pounding in my temple. I was hot, and I could hear my breath drawing deep like I was climbing a hill. Someone patted me on the back, but I waved it off without releasing my fixed stare at Calvin.

"Ready?"

"Ready!" I struck with confidence, trying to will the pain in my arm into Calvin's shoulder and through him. Calvin had tightened his muscle for the hit, but the muscles gave way against my knuckles and I knew he felt it. I felt it too, with a shock that ran up my arm to the shoulder joint as if he was hitting my fist with his shoulder instead of the other way around. But he stopped smiling.

"Ready?"

I wiped sweat from my forehead and said, "Ready!" But I wasn't. Being a lefty, I was getting hit in the same arm I was hitting with and the arm was going numb. My fingers tingled and weakness was spreading up from there. In spite of that, my fist clenched and wanted another chance, but Calvin's second blow sent me spinning to the ground where my cheek felt the gravel. I cussed, not because I was down, but because I was out just when my arm was reaching for more.

Someone grabbed me and helped me to my feet. It was David. "Are you nuts?" he said. "We shouldn't be here! This is trouble. Big-time trouble! Bad shit!"

I scrambled to my feet and brushed him off, then strutted stiffly out of the circle of boys. "Just a game, man, just a game." Someone handed me a bottle, and I took a swig of something that burned my throat, maybe tequila. "Time to grow up, Davy boy. I can slug with these guys."

"Yeah, right. I can see that." He pushed me down on the steps of the temporary classroom.

I grinned up at his friendly, concerned face. "I won one. And I'll win again. What are you doing here? I thought you were working that new girl."

"Yeah, that. She went home with some friends. I guess I'm on the market again. I don't think we were much of a match."

"Maybe you want to punch somebody."

David laughed. "Yeah, right on!" But he walked away from the circle and found a place on the wall.

The sluggers continued, and I watched them instead of listening to David. "This is it!" I yelled.

He wouldn't quit ragging on me though. "Yeah, it's the thing all right. Until you get busted," he said, circling back for another try. "The teachers know about this and you can't afford any more write-ups."

Calvin went through three guys before Phelps came in and finished him.

Phelps was flushed and leering. "Where's the southpaw hippie?" he yelled. The crowd turned and looked for me. It was getting dark though, and the faces were hard to see in the shadow of the building.

"Come on, Barger!" someone yelled.

"I'm here," I said, stepping forward with my chin out.

"Barger?" said Phelps. "Saw your picture in the paper, right? I bet Joe's pissed."

"Leave my brother out this, Phelps." I came into the circle and stood nose to nose with him again.

Phelps turned to the crowd. "Recognize him now, guys? Got his picture in the paper with his little protest march."

David was right behind me. "Are you crazy? Let's get out of here," he whispered.

I waved him off and clenched my teeth, feeling like I was way out of my league but too proud to back down now. Maybe only I knew that my earlier win was a fluke and my chances of repeating were somewhere between little and none. "Ready!"

I lasted through three slugs with Phelps before stumbling off the line and catching myself with one hand before I fell. He followed me, his face taunting and red. "Ya like that, huh? Ya like it down there, pizza boy?"

As I came up from the ground, he slugged me again, same

place, same shoulder. "What are you doing here, Barger? You should be jackin' off with your hippie friends!"

He was laughing when I staggered back to the line, dizzy and seriously pissed. Crazy, stupid Barger pissed. "Screw you, Phelps." My left arm hung dead at my side useless, so I hit his face with my right fist instead, splitting his lip.

"You bastard!" he growled. I never saw the fist that blacked my eye and blurred my vision even more. I was on the ground again, this time with that son-of-a-bitch on top of me. Thank god someone yelled, "Teachers!" Phelps's buddies dragged him off me, and the group scattered into the twilight.

David leaned over with hands on his knees like he was afraid to touch me. "Shit! You okay?"

"That was fun!" I said, rising shakily and confused.

"You're so full of shit you could spit turds," David said.

A cool had descended on the gravel parking lot and the scuffle of running feet was replaced by the sound of revving engines and skidding tires as the others fled the scene. Suddenly the two of us were alone.

David shook his head. "Come on!" he said. "This way!" He led me between two of the portable classrooms. We were crossing the parking lot with me staggering along behind him when Vice Principal Parker appeared out of nowhere.

"Whoa, how did you do that?" said David. "That was like Batman, the way you just stepped out of the dark." He danced nervously in front of Parker with his hands on his hips.

"I'm just that good. But I'm more like the Shadow, don't you think? And now, I think you boys are heading for a meeting in my office."

"What for?" I asked, feeling drunk and unsteady.

The vice principal smiled, stepped close, and slapped me on the left shoulder. I couldn't help but wince. "Hurt yourself dancing,

Barger?"

"No, sir. I'm good."

David spoke up. "Just headin' home, sir. That's where we were heading."

Parker gripped my shoulder then, squeezing, so I couldn't help but cringe and pull away. He looked at my buddy. "You, Mr. Nelson, you are heading home. Then Monday, report for noon detention. But Mr. Barger and I are going to do some paperwork. He won't be in school on Monday."

David shook his head and tossed me my jacket. "Come on, Parker. Give him a break." Then to me, "Be cool, man."

"Like ice." I shrugged off the hand on my shoulder and slipped on the jacket, trying not to show how much that motion hurt an arm that didn't want to move at all.

"You, Mr. Barger, are going on a little vacation for fighting on school grounds. And don't worry, I will be seeing Mr. Phelps first thing Monday morning."

I didn't speak. The shoulder was all I felt.

NINETEEN

When Joe walked out of the airport on Saturday morning, he moved like the old Joe. He was lean and tan and walked with only the slightest limp. "Hey, Humpy, good to see you behind the wheel." He wore a hooded sweatshirt, canvas work pants, and rubber boots, with a black cap pushed back off his forehead. I opened the trunk and he tossed in his duffel and a knapsack. When we shook hands, he smelled of salt and sea and fish like Dad did when we were fishing the salmon of Cook Inlet. The rich smells brought back those memories of childhood.

I had been moping around the house when Joe had called from the airport at ten in the morning wanting a ride. My wounded pride and battered muscles after my run-in with Phelps were bad enough, but then the vice principal had me mad at the world. I tried to hide my mood, but Joe noticed the black eye right away.

"Whoa there, Humpy, what's this? Your girlfriend do this to you?" He laughed.

"You oughta see the other guy."

"Attaboy! I thought you were a lover, not a fighter."

"I didn't have much choice. It was that guy Phelps. You know him. He's an asshole. Unfortunately, he's a pretty good fighter too."

"I remember that shithead." Joe patted my shoulder, making me wince. But I would swallow my tongue before showing I felt it. "So, you got your license?" he asked.

"Yeah, I took your advice and just did it. In fact, I didn't tell Mom until just now when you called. Of course, she was already in her robe and slippers when the phone rang, so I just said, 'I'll go, Mom.' She gave me a dirty look, but that was all."

Joe laughed. I liked how that sounded. He had me stop at a liquor store where he bought a case of beer. He finished one by the time we got home and I had my guard up again.

Mom made leftover meatloaf sandwiches. Joe started talking while he put catsup on his sandwich. He had been working on fish tender, buying fish from the fishermen and hauling it to the cannery. The skipper didn't drink and wouldn't let his crew drink either. All summer Joe had sent short notes on postcards from towns like Homer, Seward, and Cordova saying he was all right and not to worry. Now here he was, sober, fit, and jovial. Just the talk of fish and boats brought back the memory of beach fishing with Dad so long ago.

"Could you get me a job like that sometime?" I asked. I wanted the smell of Dad with the beach all on his clothes again.

"I tell you what, Sam," Joe said around a mouthful of food. "I know you love fishing, but boat work is tough. All that lifting and hauling for long hours, and the floor is always rockin'. Sleeping in a damp bunk that reeks of fish and motor oil and other men's farts."

I laughed.

"Yeah, you laugh, but if you're smart you'll study hard and find another line of work."

"So, how in the world were you able to do work like that?" Mom ventured.

I wanted to yell at her, *He's better. Can't you tell?* All the tension from last spring was gone and we were together at the table having a civil conversation, and now here Mom was, picking scabs.

"I couldn't at first," he said. "They made me cook and bookkeeper, and then I kinda eased into the heavy work through the summer."

"So, you're better?"

"Oh, I'm still slow and weak, but I'm getting there. Hard work, Mom," said Joe. "Like you always said, 'Nothing like hard work to calm the mind.'" I wanted to freeze this moment with the three of us there at the table with the past left behind and future full of hope.

"I'm not as dumb as you think I am. Am I?" she answered, and we all laughed. "What are you going to do now that the season is over? Will you stay around?"

"Already got something lined up, but first I got to take my little brother hunting."

"What do you mean?" I asked. Was I finally hearing what I had waited for all summer?

Joe reached for the last piece of meatloaf, cut it in half, and forked one part onto my plate. Then he got up and fetched another beer. "Huntin', kid," he said. "We gotta get you hunting. The Bargers are good at two things: work and hunting. It's in the blood."

Mom turned her attention on me then. "You know your brother got suspended from school?" she said. "He's had quite a week."

"Wouldn't have something to do with that black eye, would it?" Joe looked at me while he chewed.

"Obviously! Fighting on school grounds. Not to mention that Mr. Big Shot got his picture in the paper *protesting*. Apparently, he didn't learn anything from his shenanigans a couple of years ago."

"I saw that picture," said Joe. "That's even better than the breaking and entering episode back in junior high. This time at least they gave you credit." That was Joe. I knew he was pissed at me, but he wouldn't just come out and say it, so he made a joke. That was making me nervous. He even changed the subject.

"You still tending the oven at that pizza joint?" Joe said, winking at me.

I shook my head. This was still Joe after all.

Mom smiled in a way that made her shoulders relax, and she reached out to pat him on the forearm. "Now about this hunting thing. You don't need to do that. I don't think either of you is ready for that sort of thing." She probably didn't want to think of us alone together, especially with both of us armed.

"Mom, a Barger is always ready to go hunting. Right, kid? You hippies ain't against huntin', are ya? I see you're even wearing the symbol of the great American chicken."

"It's a peace symbol, Joe. I'm not a hippie. I'm just me. You probably want to go hunting so you can shoot me."

Joe laughed. Mom didn't. "Samuel Barger," she said, "I don't want to hear any kind of talk like that. Shame on you. But the guns, Joe," she added. "I worry about the guns."

"If there is anyone who knows about guns, it's me. Christ, Mom. That's one thing I'm good at."

"Joseph! Your language."

"Come on, Ma, don't change the subject," he said. "I know what I'm doing. I'm a Marine, and every Marine is a rifleman. And that's on top of what Pop already taught me. Trust me, Mom. It'll be fine. And Sam knows what he's doing. We're not a couple of kids anymore."

I knew Joe wouldn't win that fight. She used to worry about Dad taking us out on the boat. With that in the past, she would find something else to fret about. "I'm just concerned. I'm your mother. It's my job to worry."

Joe kept talking. "And my old rifle is still here. And you still have the Model 71 Dad gave you, don't you?" He turned to me. "Remind me to tell you that story some time."

Mom slapped his arm. "You will do no such thing. Some things are better left alone." Then she went to the kitchen muttering under her breath.

"Okay, Mom. My lips are sealed." He winked at me again, and I knew then it was my turn.

I reached in my pocket and pulled out the key to the '57. I had found a rabbit's foot key ring at the pawnshop next to the pizza parlor. I went there sometimes to look at the hunting knives, and I liked the idea of having the keychain for Joe when he came home. And the truck was almost running. I tossed it across the table to Joe and it skidded off the edge and dropped to the floor.

"What's this?" He picked up the keys and juggled them like they were hot.

"The '57, Joe. She's all ready for you. It's ready, battery and everything. I think it just needs a tune-up. She fires but won't run."

"I had a girl like that once." Joe sat back in his chair and grinned. "Damn, Humpy, you finally got your shit together. Now you just gotta carry it."

I didn't say a damn thing. I wanted to crawl in a hole somewhere and nurse my wounds. I was way beyond letting him get to me.

By noon the next day, Joe and his buddy Frank were out at the GMC with a six-pack and the hood up. I watched through the window as they tinkered and laughed around the truck I couldn't get running. Just like David said, in fifteen minutes they had it started with the engine humming as the two men stood together looking under the hood. Joe patted Frank on the back, and they toasted with their beer cans.

Joe stomped into the house and called for me. "Come on, Humpy. Let's you, me, and Frank take the truck for a spin, maybe go shoot something." I wanted to say no, but somehow I couldn't.

TWENTY

A gravel pit on the bluff overlooking Cook Inlet was a makeshift shooting range, and that's where Joe took us for target practice. We set up cardboard targets on a rickety metal table that was once part of someone's kitchen and now sat in the middle of thousands of spent brass cartridges and shotgun shells. Fifty yards away, two other men were already shooting at coffee cans they had lined up on a log.

Joe patted me on the back. "Wanna build us a fire and take some of this chill off the air?" he asked.

"Sure," I said. "Wouldn't want Frank to get his hands dirty." No one heard me so I went off with the hatchet to attack a broken pallet riddled with bullet holes. Then I found a dead spruce that had fallen off the edge of the gravel bank. I hacked off several branches and dragged them back to a ring of rocks that had been a fire ring before.

Joe liked a campfire and he had his particular way of building one. He had taught me one weekend out on the banks of the Susitna River when he had buried his Mustang up the axles in river mud. It started spitting rain that day and the wind chilled us down. "This car's going nowhere right now," Joe had said. "Let's build a fire and warm up." That day he showed me each step. "First, you dry fuel, especially to get it started." He led me to a spruce tree and broke off an armload of dead branches from around the bottom of the trunk. "See, this squaw kindling will be dry when everything else is wet. Even when it's raining it'll stay dry 'cause it's protected by the branches above. And you can break it off 'cause it's brittle. That's your kindling. Then, if you got it, birch bark is the best tinder. It's loaded with pitch and the bark will burn even soaking wet."

He looked around. "Next thing you need is a base," Joe said. "Branches about the size of your arm."

I'd hustled off to collect driftwood the right size. "Some of these are damp," I said.

"No matter. They'll dry." Then he made a platform. "This keeps the fire off the wet ground while it gets started." Finally, Joe broke up a wad of kindling and built a tripod of the larger pieces of squaw kindling. "Slip your tinder in and light it up. Good, hot fire guaranteed."

I remembered this now as I used the piece of pallet for my platform and built the tripod out of dead spruce branches. I didn't have any birch bark but there were plenty of paper plates lying around. I slipped a roll of paper plates into the wad of sticks and reached for my matches. I had none.

"In over your head there, kid?" asked Frank. He and Joe had paced off a hundred yards to the targets and set up the table with cartridges and rifles.

"Just need a light."

"Here!" Joe tossed me a shotgun shell.

"Gunpowder?" I asked. Then I saw it was a spent twelve-gauge shotgun cartridge with a smaller twenty-gauge pushed inside it so they made a tight case. I pulled them apart and the case was full of matches.

"Keep it," Joe said. "You'll need it when we go hunting."

"Thanks." I selected a match and struck it on a rock. The paper lit quickly, and in minutes the fire was blazing.

I could feel and hear the rumble of the heavy hunting rifles the other men were firing. The smell of gunpowder was thick. I nodded my head through all the instructions Joe recited. "Never point your gun at anyone. Treat every gun as a loaded gun. Guns are only dangerous when people act stupid. Only shoot at something you want to kill."

"Come on, Joe. You act like I never handled a gun before."

"Okay, okay. You see, kid," said Joe in a serious businesslike voice, "this is all stuff I learned in the service—and from Dad. Every season you need to sight in your rifle so you know it's shooting straight, and you are shooting straight. Those targets are about a hundred yards off. That's as far as you want to be shootin' at moose if you want to hit it." I winced when he patted me on the shoulder. "You okay?"

"Fine." I shook the arm to loosen it. The bruise wasn't bad, but it was sensitive to the touch. "Let's shoot."

"Okay, but I'm serious about the safety business. Guys have been shot and killed when some idiot got careless."

Then came the firing instructions. "Three nice deep breaths, then exhale slowly as you sight and squeeze the trigger. Nice and slow," he said. I thought the shooting was going to be easy at such a big target. Then when I put the rifle to my shoulder and looked at it through the peep sight on the Model 71, the target seemed to shrink. I squeezed the trigger. After the first two shots hit the corner of the big black X, I fired five rounds without hitting the target at all. I don't think I even hit the cardboard box. I rubbed my tender shoulder where the gun had slammed back each time I fired.

Frank laughed. "Son, you have never experienced the kick of a big rifle." I glared at him. This kind of lesson was supposed to be just me and Joe. I didn't need a stupid jarhead running commentary.

"I didn't tell you, but this is a tree buster of a rifle," Joe said. "That .348 cartridge packs a wallop. I'm impressed with how you're handling it. You know what to expect from it now. It won't surprise you." Then he showed me how to hold the gun tight so the recoil would spread through my body instead of hitting the shoulder like a blow from a baseball bat.

Frank leaned on the table and snickered, then he reached under the table and opened a case of beer. He had a can halfway to his mouth when Joe yelled at him. "No way, jarhead! No drinking on my rifle range. Stow the beer."

Frank looked disgusted and threw the can of beer downrange. He pulled a pistol from a holster on his belt and fired three fast rounds. The can bounced once and spewed beer. "I still got it, baby!" whooped Frank. The two of them laughed then.

"Not sure what *it* is," said Joe with a chuckle.

I watched the two men shoot round after round, reloading and firing, slowly and carefully reloading, sighting, breathing, and firing, while I counted the tiny holes appearing around the black center of the X. I could imagine them then—two young men in green fatigues halfway around the world, shooting rats before a battle. Mom thought Joe would have had enough of guns and shooting, but these two guys seemed pretty comfortable to me. I wandered off and collected more wood for the fire.

Joe made me reload and shoot twenty more times. I started hitting the target, but my shoulder was like hamburger, as if it wasn't bad enough before.

When my final round of shots all struck within four inches of the center, even Frank was impressed. "Attaboy, Sam. Attaboy. You nailed it!"

"I guess I did, didn't I?"

"Yup, you sure did. Just remember. Safety is always first," said Joe. "Hokey as it sounds."

"I'm no idiot, Joe."

"I know that. But this is nothing you can ever relax about." We each fired a few more rounds before Joe said, "Let's pack it in. It's beer-thirty."

We slid the rifles into their cases and Joe made Frank put his pistol in the glove box. "You need a window rack for that GMC," said Frank.

"I'll get around to it," Joe said. Only then did Joe crack three beers and pass them around. As soon as we'd had one sip of beer, the two of them settled into a soft chatter without the tension that came with shooting. I leaned on a fender and watched them.

Frank reached into his coat and brought out a pint bottle of whiskey. He pointed at me. "That brother of yours is the reason I'm here. Did you know that?"

I shook my head and wished him gone.

He opened the bottle and drank. "I don't mean here at the shooting range. I mean here on this earth. He's the reason."

"Ah, Frank. Don't start. Don't talk about 'Nam," said Joe. I walked away to retrieve our cardboard targets and Frank's shot-up beer can.

"Oh no. I ain't shuttin' up. Your hippie kid brother here needs to know what it's all about. This kid needs to know who his brother is, who he really is." Frank passed the bottle.

"I know all I need to know," I said. I started tearing the cardboard boxes and tossing pieces on the fire.

"Whoa!" said Frank. "Hey, show some respect, punk! Oh, that's right. You're the hippie of the family. Always protesting something."

"I ain't protesting, Frank. Just speakin' my mind. Remember free speech? Isn't that part of what you were fighting for?"

"Yeah. I remember, kid, so shut up and listen."

Joe chimed in, "Easy, Frank." He pulled hard on the bottle and passed it on to Frank.

"Yeah, yeah. You see, kid—"

"Sam, the name's Sam." Shooting with him and sharing beers wasn't making me like this guy anymore. I wanted to walk away to show the man that I wasn't interested, that I didn't care, but I stayed and listened.

"Okay, Sam! Anyway, your brother was my platoon partner in 'Nam. I was at the end of my tour, but it turns out he took care of me . . . and brought me home. He took care of all of us.

"I remember this one kid in our squad. He was all of about eighteen years and fifteen minutes but looked younger 'n you, just a peach-fuzz kid. That's what we called him, Peach. That kid's green as asparagus like we all was when we hit that hole. So one day we was out on patrol, humpin' through the heat o' the day, when the sarge calls a halt. 'Take a quarter,' he says. So we all flop down like we was dead. The sarge points to Peach. 'Your turn to take watch. Move down the trail a ways and keep your eyes open.' Peach says, 'What the hell, sarge? Me again? Why always me? I'm tired too, you know.' Sarge says, 'Tired? Why you tired? What are you carryin'? Jaybird's got the radio. Rice has the mortar, and Frank has the mortar ammo. Barger's got the BAR, and you ain't carryin' shit! Now get out there!' Well, this kid was hot and stupid . . . kinda like you, come to think of it. 'What about you, sarge?' he says. 'What are you carryin'?'

"Your brother never even raised his voice. He just leaned over and put his hand on the kid's arm. 'Sarge is carryin' you, asshole,' he said. 'In fact, he's carryin' all of us. All damn day, every day.' I never laughed so hard in my life. Well, Peach shut his damn mouth and slinks out to take his sentry position.

"Five minutes later we hear a shot and Peach screams. He's lyin' there howling like a stuck pig. He's yelling, 'Corpsman, corpsman!

Help me, I'm hit!' Well, Joe here is up like the sun and goes flying after Peach and rolls him into the brush. He lies on top of him and covers his mouth until the rest of us can clean up the sniper. Turns out the kid was okay. The round hit his flack jacket after it done went through a tree or something. Just left a good welt. Your brother wasn't so lucky. Not just getting shot, but getting shot where he did. And he never tried to explain it to anybody, just dealt with all the crap. But if it hadn't been for your brother, that sniper would have got Peach for sure.

"But instead, that guy, Peach, went on to outlast all of us, and I heard he won a medal for saving his whole platoon. Just 'cause of your brother keepin' him alive to fight another day. Your brother is the Man. Shit, I'd die for him. Hell, I'd kill for him. Better be good to your brother, or I'll get ya." Frank shook an empty beer at me and then threw it over his shoulder.

Joe chuckled, and the three of us sat silently for a moment looking into the fire. "You just never know," said Frank. "You just never know."

"I wish you'd quit telling that story," said Joe. "We gotta leave that behind." He struggled to his feet and moved around stiffly.

"Behind is right!" Frank laughed. "Stories help me."

"Forgetting helps me."

"Yeah, right. Forget you."

"Forget who?"

They both laughed and I felt like an intruder. I was resenting Frank more and more. This was supposed to be my time with Joe. Instead, I got a big-mouth Frank in the bargain.

"Wanna hear about this gun, the 71 Winchester?" asked Joe.

"Sure," said Frank. It was a story Joe was going to tell me, but now he was telling Frank. I was pushed to the side, just along for the ride.

"Well, it was back when things were tight," Joe began. "Sometimes Dad would go off on a toot and have a couple too many, then he'd come back and try to get back in Mom's good graces. He'd usually bring her candy or flowers, something nice. One night he walks in with this rifle. I think it was the week before his heart attack. He and Mom had been squabbling, and he waved his white handkerchief like a flag of truce. 'I brought you a peace offering.' He held out the gun to Mom, and she was dumbfounded. 'What am I supposed to do with that?' she asked. He said, 'Well, to go hunting with me, or . . . you could use it on me next time I piss you off.' He laughed his come-on-I'm-a-nice-guy laugh.

"Now, Mom didn't think that was funny at all. 'Don't even talk like that!' she said, pissed as all get out. But you know. In the end, she forgave him, not for everything of course. But she didn't begrudge him buying a gun he didn't need and she would never use. The gun just stood in the closet since that day."

The two laughed and nodded like it was the perfect way for things to be. "Now it's Sam's rifle," Joe said. "And here we are." He spread his arms like he was embracing the world. "And you are ready! Sam. Let's go hunting!" The liquor was in him again and he showed something else—something that was more than the liquor. The other Joe was back.

"Big-ass rifle for a kid," said Frank. He opened another beer. "Especially a hippie boy like you, kiddo."

"Up yours, Frank. The name's Sam," I said. "I'm not a hippie, and what the hell do you know about hippies anyway?"

"Whoa! You sure look like a hippie to me with that long hair and jewelry," Frank said, and he waved his beer in my direction. "I'll tell you what I know, *Sam*. I know I was with your brother when we hobbled off the plane in San Francisco and your hippie brethren were spitting at us and calling us murderers. I know you damn kids need to figure out that thanks to what we do, you can march and wear long hair and beads like a bunch of girls. I know if you was my brother, you'd show a little more respect or get your ass kicked."

I was stupid and Barger enough to take a challenge like that, so I jumped up and stuck my chin out. "Any time you're ready, big mouth!"

Frank didn't even set down his beer. "Don't let nothing stop you but fear and common sense." I was way beyond both of those.

Joe was watching us both warily. "All right, Sam. Easy does it. Get off your high horse." He turned to Frank. "Jesus, Frank. Put a cork in it." I stalked off and picked up our spent brass cartridges off the ground. Frank stood with his hands on his hips and watched Joe as he kicked gravel into the remains of the campfire.

Joe was on the other side of the truck stowing the guns when I wandered back with my hands full of spent cartridges, wondering how many spent cartridges there were scattered around Vietnam. Frank came up beside me.

"Well, goddamnit," he said. "You and me better make up or Joe'll kick both our asses." He kicked the ground nervously. "I love your brother, man. He is . . . He is that guy you always want beside you whether you're in deep shit or havin' a party. He's the guy you want with you." He put out his hand.

"Yeah, okay." I was still mad, but not stupid fighting-mad anymore. I shook his hand. Frank didn't let go.

"He cares about you, Sam. And he feels this big duty to fill in for your dad. When we was over there in the jungle, we'd get homesick and sad, and then he'd suck it up and say, 'Frank, we gotta do this right so Sam don't have to go through this crap.' He don't want you to have to go over there and be in that."

I thought that sounded made up, like something John Wayne would have said in *The Green Berets*. "Must have been nasty," I said. "Joe doesn't say much."

"You don't even want to know. If you meet some guy coming back all braggin' and tellin' badass gung-ho war stories, you'll know he was never in the shit. Not really. He mighta been in the country, but he'd never been in *it.* 'Cause guys who've been in it, really in it, they don't say much. 'Cept me, I guess. I talk too much."

I nodded.

Joe said, "You two ready to go?"

He didn't know how ready I was. I was ready to be gone from Joe and Frank and Mom, all of it. One more push and I would be totally gone. That push wasn't long in coming.

TWENTY-ONE

When Iris called that evening and wanted to hang out, I was a drowning swimmer being thrown a rope. All of the hassle with Joe and Frank was forgotten. Mom's cold shoulder and Pete's disapproval pushed out of my mind. Iris was just the salve my wounds needed.

She picked me up in her mom's sedan, gave me a little kiss, and said, "I got some pot. Let's go get high."

The evening was cool and cloudy, so there was no one around our little spot in the park where we sat under a tree in our sweatshirts. She lit the joint and passed it to me. I was sucking in the smoke and tasting the sweet mustiness of it when she gasped. "My God, Sam! Your eye!"

I exhaled and coughed. "It's nothin'." Like Joe, she had noticed the black-and-blue half-moon that had formed under my right eye and a small cut just to the right of the eyebrow. I was surprised she hadn't seen it before but was glad for the sympathy.

"Ahh, what happened?" She touched me gently and kissed the black-and-blue eye. "That looks nasty."

I drew a deep toke on the joint for dramatic effect. "I got punched," I said.

If I had stopped there, I would have been just fine. But a guy's pride gets in his way sometimes. *I got punched* sounds like I was some wimp getting picked on by a bully. How manly is that? So I told her the whole story of my sordid Friday night. Well, not the whole story. "I got goaded into this stupid slugging game," I said. "Then this prick, a guy I had to throw out of the pizza parlor"—yes, I exaggerated—"he took it personally and it turned into a fight." I tried to make to look like I was more of a victim of circumstance than I really was. "I had to defend myself," I said. The pot was making me lightheaded and confident.

She took the joint and drew deep on it. "That doesn't sound like you, Sam. Fighting like that."

Even at this point I had a chance to salvage the situation, but I got cocky. I l lay back against the tree and looked at the changing leaves on the birches along the lake. Most of them had turned to gold coins and they drifted to earth a few at time. "Sometimes, Iris, you just react when people push you too far," I said. "Guys like Phelps, they think they can run over people. You gotta stand up to them. I was sick of that pissant."

"No you don't. You don't have to stoop to his level. You could just walk away. That's a peace symbol you're wearing, remember." She stood up and crossed her arms. I stood too, reaching for her.

"Oh, come on! That's not how it works. It's like karate or judo. They talk about the way of peace and avoiding conflict, but then they teach you how to fight, how to defend yourself. That's me."

"Oh, now you're some badass martial arts expert?" She brushed off my hand and turned her back.

"No, no. That's not what I mean. I'm trying to say that sometimes you have to stand your ground. Come on," I said, "it's no big deal." Note: don't tell someone who's already pissed off, *It's no big deal.* I reached out and tried to kiss her, but she pushed me away. Obviously even the pot wasn't going to mellow her out.

"Quit it, Sam. Don't even try to charm your way out of this. You're just trying to change the subject. If you're for nonviolence, you have to live it. And that whole stupid slugging game? What are you, fourth graders?"

"It's not like I'm fighting all the time," I said. "I just got pushed into a corner. Shit! I can't please anybody."

And then she was gone. The brown eyes, the freckles, and all that wit and energy and laughter went with her when she got up and walked to the car. She wasn't just gone either. She was *gone.* There was something about the way she walked, or the look she gave before she left, but something told me there was no going back. I didn't even try to follow.

It's not totally accurate to say Iris broke up with me. We weren't really going steady in the first place, and I'm sure she would tell you we were "just hangin' out." Even though we had spent a lot of time together and had some pretty heavy make-out sessions. Anyway, when she drove off in her car, I knew she was off limits to me for the time being.

Of course, at first I was disgusted that she was being so narrow minded. Couldn't she sympathize with a guy being cornered like I was? A man had to be a man, didn't he? No matter what Martin Luther King, Jr., Gandhi, and Jesus said, you can't always turn the other cheek.

I sat under that tree by the lake, wounded, angry, and totally alone. Being a little stoned probably didn't help. I wanted to run through the woods screaming, and I wanted to sit there and cry like a kid. I started walking instead, not walking home—just walking. I followed the path along the lake and replayed the conversation. I realized how cocky I sounded, full of wind and swagger. What an idiot! I sounded like Joe.

I knew then what I could have said, even if it was a bit of a lie. I could have said I got caught up in something and how foolish I felt. I could have played down the tough-guy part. But I didn't, and now I was walking through the woods alone instead of making out under a birch tree. I was listening to the empty forest instead of the tinkle of her words. I was alone. Worse than that, I couldn't see tomorrow. I couldn't see us at the lunch table with me cleaning up her sandwich bones and making her laugh and punch my shoulder. I couldn't see us talking about the war and women's rights, and who's going to be president. I couldn't see us making out with her small breast in my hand and slowly unbuttoning the fly on her cutoffs. None of that was possible. Tomorrow was an empty bucket. I couldn't even see us back where we started, *just buds.*

When I'd feel like this, full of maudlin self-pity, I'd get a longing for the cabin on the bluff and the times when Dad was alive. I wished I was a kid again who didn't know how shitty the world could be. I had foolishly dreamed that I could have the girl, that I could be the rebel who changed the world, that I could fix my brother. None of that seemed possible now. And my silly idea about making peace with Joe and hunting up a moose together was the biggest stupid idea of all.

A loon was cruising the lake and I heard its call, but not the mournful and haunting call. All I heard was the foolish, high-pitched chuckle that ridiculed me, and I took a mental detour to wonder if that's where the word "loony" came from.

A loony plan began to form in my head, but the pot I smoked had filled my brain with fog, so I sat under a tree listening to the loon until I fell asleep. The nap was deep and filled with confusing dreams of moose hunting with Iris in Delaney Park and Joe chasing us. He was dressed in full battle gear, and I was carrying a sign that I couldn't read. I ran—that crazy, hopeless dream run that happens in slow motion so that no matter how fast I ran, I wasn't getting anywhere. I woke up cold and disoriented. Then I remembered how I ended up there in the dark by the lake with a loon laughing at me.

I gathered what was left of my wits and walked the two miles home, thinking the whole way that I needed to make a big move. I didn't need Joe or Iris or any of this shit that was holding me back. The fog had lifted, and the idea that I had before I fell asleep was growing stronger and driving me forward.

TWENTY-TWO

By nine o'clock the next morning, I was standing on the Seward Highway with my pack on my back and my thumb in the air. It was a cool Monday morning with a hint of winter soon to come, so I was bundled in a wool coat and hat and wearing gloves. My pack had a sleeping bag, some canned food, and a change of clothes. When a station wagon pulled over I climbed into a warm seat with a middle-aged man with a cigarette hanging out of the corner of his mouth. Through the smoke of his Camel, he eyed the Model 71 I had rolled in a blanket and tied with shoestrings. "That gun empty?"

"Yup."

"You can put it in the backseat there. Where you headed?"

"Ninilchik," I said. "I'm going back home."

"Home's a good place to go."

"You're damn right," I said, and we left Anchorage at sixty miles an hour.

My ride didn't have much to say, and I was busy thinking how pissed Mom would be when she read the note I left her. Pete wasn't happy either when I had made that hard phone call, telling him I was going moose hunting since I had a few days off school. "You didn't give me much warning," he had said, "but you covered for me enough time last summer. Don't forget to come back, but don't be gone long."

I wasn't leaving for good, I had told him, and I told myself I wasn't running away from anything. I was running *to* something, to our old cabin, to go moose hunting. If I stayed in town I'd be calling Iris and making an ass of myself while she was still pissed at me. If I let her cool off, she might remember the good times we had. I sure hoped so. That's as far as I thought ahead for a change and that was a big step for me, heading off without big ambitious dreams in my head.

I got to the bluff by midafternoon and walked down the lane with my pack and the rifle under my arm. The place was all the same as I remembered, but somehow also completely different. The cabin still stood in the trees with its three-sided logs and the board and batten shop set back away from it. But I remembered light and warmth, smoke in the chimney, snowdrifts rising over my head, and the long walk down a tunnel of snow to the outhouse. Now, on this cloudless fall day, the place was cold and compressed, smaller and settled closer to the ground, so the cabin was a chilled hovel where only the most desperate souls might linger. The wind stirred the treetops and rattled the dead leaves clinging to the birches. I pulled my coat closer.

Windows were black in the falling light, and the dying pushki plants standing against the dark logs gave the place a sad and sinister feel. For the last few miles I had been anticipating being there, starting a fire in the woodstove and setting up a simple camp. There were books left behind as I remembered, and mattresses without bedding. I was home for the first time in two years. Maybe I wouldn't leave. Maybe I'd find someone who needed some firewood split or coal hauled from the beach, and I'd barter for canned salmon or moose burger and spend days in the woods and become the outdoorsman I always wanted to be as a kid.

I turned the knob on the front door and nearly fell when my boots set me skidding across the linoleum. I laughed, remembering that cold floor on winter mornings and how boots slid out from under me when I dashed in without thinking. I imagined the smell of coffee and wood smoke, heard the burble of the percolator and the crackle of spruce kindling in the firebox of the woodstove.

I visited each of the five rooms cut in the narrow rectangle of the log cabin Dad had built for us to grow up in. It felt colder inside than out, and I was glad to find an armload of firewood beside the stove and a fire laid in the stove waiting for a match. Joe must've done that. A full jar of Strike-Anywhere matches sat on the shelf, so I lit a gold flash in my hand and dropped a match in the open lid of the stove. I watched the flames grow and thought how Joe would have readied this the last time he left the place, just like Dad would. Dad used to do the same thing in the beach cabin. "Always leave a fire ready to go and matches at hand so you or somebody else can warm the place quickly without scrounging for firewood, just in case," Dad would say. "If it's not an emergency, it's a lucky convenience."

While the cabin warmed, I unpacked my clothes in our old bedroom. I was glad to do this alone, to return without the burden of words and shared reflections. The cabin and all it meant to my childhood was a different place now, and I needed to figure that out. I didn't need Joe's drunken drama thrown in. I carried the food to the kitchen and found a saucepan and a skillet with four plates, two saucers, a couple of soup bowls, and six coffee cups.

In the pantry closet were a half can of Hills Bros coffee, a gallon jar of flour, one of oatmeal, and another of dried beans. A dozen cans of vegetables survived a couple of winters, but I grimaced at the thought of eating them after being frozen and thawed so many times. There was a shaker of salt and one of pepper. In the same closet, what I thought was a broom handle was a gun barrel. The gun surprised me, but I brought it out of the closet and leaned it the corner of the living room. A twenty-gauge pump.

When the cabin warmed enough that I could shed my coat and hat, I fed the stove again, then heated a can of soup from my pack and ate while leafing through an encyclopedia. The whole twenty-six-volume set was still on the shelf along with a collection of novels. I wasn't ready to sleep, so I looked through the books that filled the rest of the shelf. I started on *Tarzan of the Apes,* reading into the night hunched on a chair by the fire with a candle and a flashlight creating a mixed halo on the pages. As I read, I could hear Dad's voice bringing the story to life and filling the house with the howl of apes and the bugle of elephants.

I woke up disoriented, fully clothed and tangled in the quilts with the book dropped to the floor. The cabin had gone cold, so I built another fire. Then I read until daylight worked its way into midmorning. When the sun hit the yard, I set out to explore.

I followed a game trail that crossed the clearing and entered the woods. After about a hundred yards the woods opened, and I looked across a wide expanse of bog with a pond in the center. It was a shorter walk than when Joe and I had last sat on the shore and watched loons. A pair of white shapes floated there like miniature icebergs. The icebergs stretched and flapped with a laughing cackle, then took a running start across the water and flew. "Swans," I whispered as if my voice might disturb the moment. Beginning with a loop around the clearing, they spiraled upward, and with a thrust of wings they were away. I watched the slow, steady motion of them until they grew dark, small, and silent. Then I walked back to the cabin.

The woodshed was half full of spruce and birch rounds, dry and knotty with curls of bark twisting away from the wood. In the corner was a small heap of beach coal, about a wheelbarrow load. The coal was in chunks the size that I would have been sent to collect off the beach and throw in the back of the Jeep while Dad and Joe collected chunks so big they had to be broken with a sledgehammer. I hefted a couple, trying to recall where and when I might have collected them. We always threw a couple of lumps of coal on the fire before going to bed, something I'd forgotten last night. The smell of coal smoke came back to me and other memories with it, and I was suddenly small and alone in that shadowed woodshed. "Damn, Sam," I said, and shook my head to clear it as I tromped out and around the shed looking for tools.

I found a splitting wedge but no sledgehammer or maul to strike it with and no ax for chopping kindling. In the rafters of the woodshed, I found snowshoes and a wooden toboggan that I remembered using to haul firewood to the house. Now that I was full sized, I chuckled to see the short distance it actually was to the house, a little ashamed at how I would complain about the chore. Hanging from a nail was a kerosene lantern, and I took it down and shook it. Empty. I set it on the woodpile, recalling the poor light I'd had for reading the night before. Maybe there was kerosene in the shop.

The shop was a low-frame building with a tarpaper roof built flat on the ground. Dad had kept room open to pull in a car that needed work. The rest was for storing fishing gear. It was strange to see it sitting empty, a hollow shell filled with the smell of the beach hauled up in the nets and rain gear that once hung here through the winter. The floor was stained with crankcase oil, and old tools and car parts hung from nails around the walls like artwork in a gallery. One broken window framed the Iliamna Volcano across the inlet so perfectly that it could have been an oil painting. I was briefly captured by the view and stepped back and forth to align the perfect framing of the scene. This was my father's place. Here and the beach were the places he left his prints. Leaning against the wall by the back door stood a rusty single blade ax and beside it a sledgehammer with a broken handle.

I found a twenty-gauge shotgun shell in the drawer of the workbench. "This will fit that gun in the house, Sam," I said to myself. It was dirty and the metal base was corroded, but I could read the shot count on the yellow sleeve. Rubbing the worst of the dirt off, I slipped the cartridge in my pocket where I could cup it in my hand and be comforted by the feel of it. I stood looking out through that window at the volcano, imagining the smell of bacon cooking in the kitchen until my stomach pulled me back to the house. On the way, I stopped at the woodshed and used the ax to fill a wheelbarrow with split firewood and kindling.

I was just making a morning coffee when a green Dodge pickup pulled up in front of the cabin. The man who got out looked familiar, but it took me some time to realize who it was. He was reaching to knock on the door when I opened it.

"Morning," I said.

"I saw the light and the tracks on the lane, so I thought I'd better check on the place," he said. "You're one of the Barger boys?" It was half statement, half question.

"Yeah, I'm Sam. Come in."

"I'm Art Mitkof. You might not remember me. I was a friend of your Dad. I told your mom I'd keep an eye on the place."

"Come on in. I just made coffee."

He stepped in and sat in a folding chair by the window, and looked around at the cabin and at me and the makeshift bed. "You here on your own? Shouldn't you be in school?"

I handed him a cup of black coffee. "I'm taking a break."

"I see. You mean moose hunting, I'd bet."

"Thinking about it." That reminded me: I had forgotten to carry the rifle when I walked out to the pond.

"How's your mom? She know where you are?" His voice was suspicious. He drank the coffee in one swallow.

I told him as little as possible. Art was a fisherman who lived about a mile down the road. He and Dad used to help each other repair outboards and haul gear to the beach. He often stopped by on winter mornings, and sometimes he would be at the table drinking coffee when we kids walked out the lane to meet the school bus. Maybe I wasn't the only one missing the old times.

"You get kicked out of school or somethin'?"

"No. Just wanted to get away. You know."

"Yeah, I know. Your mom called and asked me to check on you. I'll let her know you're okay."

"Thanks. More coffee?"

"Nope. I gotta get to the beach for coal during the tide."

I should have known Mom would find some way to check on me. I guess it made sense. At least she didn't send the troopers.

This was a man who spent as much time with Jim Barger as anyone, and I wanted to ask about Dad. I wanted to beg for stories about him. Instead, we talked about the weather and fishing, and then Art put on his cap and headed for the door. He turned with his hand on the knob. "How's your brother? He healing all right? Tough thing, that. I'm thinking it's been tough for your mom too." He sighed and looked pained. "Your dad, he caused her a lot a worry too, you know. Then he died. I don't know which pissed her off the most."

"Yeah. I know." I felt an aching in my gut as I looked at the weathered fisherman and remembered Dad.

"You're young. You'll all get over it. Your mom too." He opened the door and looked out at the yard. "You need anything, come on by." And then he was gone. I sat on the folding chair, staring out at the green pickup as it backed toward the shop, turned, and moved out to the highway.

I ate oatmeal and drank weak coffee, looking out the window across Cook Inlet at the volcanoes with their white shoulders so bold against the sky. A container ship was moving up the Inlet toward Anchorage, and I thought about the beach cabin down below the bluff where I last saw Dad alive. I wanted to go there but it wasn't ours, not anymore, so I drank more coffee and wondered what Dad would think of the choices I had made.

I found myself rubbing the shotgun shell in my pocket.

I got the gun out of the pantry and dipped a rag soaked in kerosene to wipe the action and polish the wooden stock. I worked the pump up and down the barrel, then rubbed the rag into each opening and seam. Kerosene wasn't gun oil, but it would do. Finally, I took the shotgun shell from my pocket and slipped it in the chamber. I worked the action to load the yellow shell into the firing chamber, then pumped it again and ejected the shell. I repeated the routine, feeling the slick metallic action of oiled parts moving together. I imagined pulling the trigger and the lead pellets leaving the barrel with a blast of fire and odor. I got a cold chill from that and returned the shotgun shell to my pocket and hung the gun on the wood pegs above the front door. There had always been a rifle or shotgun on those pegs when I was growing up, and if I got up in the morning and the pegs were empty, I knew Dad or Joe was hunting.

Late that afternoon, I heard a vehicle and looked up, thinking Art Mitkof had returned. Instead I saw a '57 GMC pickup with an off-color fender. Joe climbed out wearing Dad's old wool hunting coat, and he stood by the truck with his hands on his hips, looking at the cabin with me staring out the dirty window.

TWENTY-THREE

"It's good to see the old place again. It doesn't look too bad."

"I thought you hated it here," I said. I'd come out on the porch to greet Joe, who was still in the yard taking in it all in. I stood on the porch in my wool socks and rubbed my arms against the cold and damp.

"Naw, I just hated fishing for Dad. Didn't even mind fishing too much, just didn't get on working for Dad." Joe chuckled. "You know, he was counting on you being the fisherman, Humpy, the way you were so eager and content on the beach. That's why your nickname Humpy stuck. He was just putting up with me until you were old enough."

"Really."

"Yeah! Too bad, huh? You got secondhand all the way around." Joe moved to the truck and pulled out a box of groceries. "I figured you were traveling light." I took the box and he leaned into the cab for his duffel. His rifle hung in a rack on the truck's back window.

I stowed the groceries while Joe walked around the cabin patting the walls and peering in closets. Then he said, "Let's go get some dinner. I could eat the ass end out of a skunk." I could smell the liquor on him and noticed how he swayed when he walked like he was still on a boat.

"Can I drive?" I asked. He tossed me the keys, and we made the drive without him asking me what hell I was doing. And I didn't ask him why the hell he followed me.

The Inlet View Cafe was an old bar and cafe that smelled of beer, cigarette smoke, and French fries like it always had. The last time I'd been there was with Dad when we had burgers and shakes one day after a good fishing period. I had sat at the bar for the first time and bummed a quarter from Dad for the jukebox while he had been bullshitting with the bartender. Now it still looked the same, but I didn't recognize the man behind the bar.

Joe said, "Sam, get us a table. I gotta piss like a racehorse." He gave the bartender a nod. "The kid's with me." We passed a payphone by the door and I fingered the coins in my pocket, wondering how much it would cost to call Iris. She would be doing homework, I figured, or maybe baking some of her oatmeal cookies. I hoped she wasn't sharing them with someone else but resisted the temptation to drop a dime and check.

I read the menu then got up and checked out the song list on the jukebox. Three guys at the bar turned on their stools and gave me the look. A guy in dirty coveralls said, "Hey, long hair. Don't play any of that rock and roll shit. Save your money for a haircut." I grinned since Elvis was the closest I saw to rock music.

"Yeah, don't think that'll be a problem," I said, heading back to my chair. I recognized two of them as men who had fished the same beach as Dad. Their names were lost to me if I ever knew them.

"We can take care of that haircut right now and save you some money. You can lose that stinkin' jewelry too," said the man in dirty coveralls who looked like he'd been at the bar all day. He was drunk and unsteady, but as tall as Joe and huskier. I was cornered, and my stomach knotted while I tried to figure out if they were just joking. I stood up just in case. I was tired of stepping back.

"Who wants to be first?" It was Joe walking in on us with a swing to his shoulders from the liquor running through him.

"What do you mean?" The man in flannel and a week-old beard took off his baseball cap and stood up, looking startled.

Joe put his hands on his hips. "Well," he said, "before you give this fellow a haircut you're going to have to whip me, so which of ya wants to go first?"

The man in coveralls said, "Hey, ain't you Jim Barger's boy?"

"That's right, and there's my little brother," said Joe. "It's been a while."

"I thought you joined up and went to 'Nam to kick some yellow ass."

"I just got back. Now I'm ready to kick some white ass right here."

"It's okay, Joe," I said. "Ain't nothing really." I was backed against the table, not knowing which way to move.

Joe was past listening though and seemed almost glad for the confrontation. The last guy, a stocky fellow who I didn't know, stood up and glared at Joe. "You reckon you can take the three of us?"

Joe reached out to steady himself on the bar. "I figure the kid can handle one of you old farts, and two of you against a live-grenade US Marine is the best you're going get. Or . . ." He let the tension fill the room with a long pause. "You could shut up and let us get our supper."

I felt the temperature going up real fast, and I wasn't sure I was as tough as Joe thought I was. Two couples having dinner at a table in the back of the room watched us and whispered back and forth across their table. But Joe wasn't done. "You ought to know," he said, "that black eye my brother's got happened the last time somebody tried to cut his hair, and you notice it never got done." I stood taller then and took a step forward, surprised and proud that Joe was standing up for me.

The stocky one, the smallest guy in the group, put his hand on the shoulder of the big man with coveralls. "Ah screw it," the stocky guy said. "Let's just give 'em some room. Shit, Joe, we're just screwing around with the kid."

The big guy didn't want to shut up or walk away. He said, "How come you don't make him cut his hair? Between that and his pretty necklace, people gonna think he's yer sister."

"That ain't none o' yer damn business," Joe said.

That made me feel me good too. But I still wanted to just get the hell out of there.

Two of the guys backed away as if they'd rather get a hold on their bottles of Oly rather than Joe Barger. I figured they were remembering Dad, and out of fear or respect they didn't want to mess with his sons.

Joe said to the big man, "It looks like your two buddies aren't interested getting bloodied over this, but if you want to go at it, it's you and me. In fact . . ." Joe suddenly pulled his knife from the sheath on his belt and stabbed it into the bar.

Roger Miller was singing on the jukebox and the twangy country song "Dang Me" filled the room, and that's all I heard for a few seconds while the big man and his buddies took an eyeful of Joe Barger, US Marine. Johnny Cash's song "A Boy Named Sue" flashed in my mind.

"This is a Marine Corps–issue Kabar fighting knife, a wicked weapon in capable hands," Joe said to the man left facing him. "You take it and I'll go empty-handed. Sound fair, old-timer?" The Kabar was the only souvenir Joe brought home from Vietnam and he kept it razor sharp. He only let me handle it once, and I could tell it made him uncomfortable when he did.

That big man looked at the knife like it was a snake that might bite him if he got to close, and then he looked at Joe. Joe hadn't moved from leaning on the bar, but his eyes were dark and his jaw was set like all that liquor in him had drained away and left nothing but meanness. I have never seen my brother battle ready before, but it was obvious he was. Hell, I'm the only person I'd ever seen him fight, but he was ready to fight now.

My hands were sweating. When I rubbed them on my pants, I felt myself shaking all over. I slipped my hands in my coat pockets then pulled them out. I didn't know if I was worried more for Joe going barehanded against a knife or that big man standing there thinking about calling his bluff. I hoped it was a bluff.

Finally, the man in the flannel said, "Jesus Christ, Tom. Come have a beer and leave the guy alone."

The big man shook his head like a boxer does when he's had his bell rung and turned away muttering, "Goddamn country's going to hell."

Joe stood there without flinching for a full minute, staring at the men's backs. Then he sheathed his knife and ordered a beer. "Whattaya wanna eat, Sam?" he said.

I had completely lost my appetite, but I made myself eat like I was ravenous. We were about finished with our hamburgers before all the anger was out of Joe's eyes. Joe cleaned his plate and said, "Damn, your hair does look like shit."

I just shook my head.

We were back at the cabin before I could talk about it. When I did I said, "Good lord, Joe, what was all that?"

Joe was feeding sticks of wood into the stove, laying them on the bed of coals left from earlier in the day. "You mean those old farts at the Inlet View? They weren't nothin'."

The fire flared up with the new fuel and cast a dancing light on the dark cabin. "Nothing? You offered the Kabar to that guy. You didn't know what he'd do? Jesus, Joe!"

"Let me tell you something, Humpy. I know a hell of a lot more about this kinda shit than you do and more than I want to.

I'll tell you, the more men talk, the less likely they are to fight. And that big guy, he's got a shotgun mouth and a BB gun ass. You know what I mean?"

I lit the kerosene lamp and hung it on the nail where it always was when we lived there. I looked at the lantern and wondered if Joe could remember those times. "Joe, what if he went for the knife? What would I do then?"

"You think I couldn't take him?"

"How was I to know? How were you to know?"

"It wasn't going to come to that, Humpy. He didn't have the stomach. Blowhard like that didn't have the brass for that kinda thing."

"But what if he did? You didn't know him."

Joe found a beer and rifled through the kitchen for an opener. Over his shoulder he said, "You might have noticed that I was standin' right next to my knife." He turned and leaned back on the counter. "If he made one move toward that knife, I'd have kicked him square in the balls. He would never touch it." Joe stood in the middle of the room like he owned it, and I couldn't meet his eyes.

I sat up late trying to read that night, but all there was to read besides an encyclopedia were Louis L'Amour Westerns. I thought maybe Joe had read too many of these from the way he acted in the bar, playing the tough gunslinger. My mind kept circling around to where me and Joe fit in this corner of this world together, and it dawned on me that Joe wasn't getting past all that he'd been through. The war had changed him, and like a guy in a wheelchair, he wasn't going to get up and walk suddenly, all clean and cured. The old Joe wasn't coming back. Even if he got past the terrors and the anger, he was different. When I turned off the lantern I didn't sleep much, and then when I woke, the last of the night still surrounded the cabin while Joe was cooking by the light of the lantern.

"Fried egg sandwiches," he said, pouring a cup of coffee and setting it within my reach. "Dad's old recipe, nothing like it anywhere."

I ignored him and walked out to the back porch to pee. All I could think of was the night before and Joe standing by that bar with the Kabar stabbed into it. The cold air slapped me awake, and I was more alert when I came back in.

"Wait till you taste them, Humpy. Shit, I mean, Sam."

"You can call me Humpy, now that I'm not one," I said, looking at the man standing at the stove like today was just another day.

"Well, Humpy. I'm going out to take a shit, and when I get back I'm going hunting. You comin'?"

We hadn't talked about hunting since he got here. He just showed up with a story of how Mom was worried, and he figured he'd take a drive down and see that I was okay. He had interrupted my escape, and then decided this should be a hunting trip. I couldn't figure out if he was trying to mend fences or just take charge. Damn it, Joe.

TWENTY-FOUR

At 9 a.m. the two Barger brothers finally loaded the rifles and climbed into the cab of the GMC pickup. In the back under a tarp were a tent, sleeping bags, a camp kitchen, and enough chow for three or four nights in the woods. We ate fried egg sandwiches and drank coffee from Dad's battered Stanley thermos bottle as I drove us along the empty highway. The egg had lots of pepper and was fried hard in bacon grease so the yolk wouldn't run. Slapped between two pieces of toasted white bread, it carried the flavor of every fried egg sandwich I'd ever eaten. I could taste the ones I ate on the edge of the cold highway while waiting for the school bus. I tasted those gobbled with a hint of beach sand down at the fish cabin. And I savored those that I'd eaten cold out of waxed paper wrappers for school lunch. I tasted all of those as I drove and listened to Joe.

"Is there anything better than a fried egg sandwich on a cold morning?" asked Joe between sips of coffee and bites of sandwich.

"Just what I was thinking. Thinking how many of these I've eaten in my life, and every damn one was just perfect."

"Nothin' like it," Joe said. He pointed at the road sign. "Ah, there's our turn."

I let off the gas and slowly turned onto Kingsley Road, then onto Oilwell Road, which was narrow and unpaved. The lights of a few houses peeked through the trees, and a light breeze pushed sprinkles of rain across the road in front of the truck's headlights.

Joe seemed relaxed and unfazed by last night's experience at the Inlet View. I couldn't get the scene out of my mind, and I wondered if I was the crazy one for going into the woods with him. Joe seemed to be thinking about everything but that. "So what happened with that little gal at the pizza parlor?" he asked. "It looked like you and her had something going."

I felt myself blush. "I told you, she's married." Besides the beer, Joe was sipping from a pint bottle he kept in his pocket, and he started talking more.

"Yeah, well, you know what they say about the married ones," he said with a laugh.

I could only shake my head. "It wasn't like that."

"That's your fault, Humpy. She was all eyeballs for you." He leaned forward to look at the ribbon of gravel road wet from heavy dew. The road was narrow and the alders hung out over it like a bower. "Pay attention here. These corners are nasty and they are banked wrong, so it's easy to slide or spin out in this rain."

"I know," I said. The pickup was light in the rear, and that was making me a little nervous. I lifted my foot off the gas and tried to resist hitting the brake. We were driving the winding slalom of corners. The next corner came up fast, and I did use the brake then. The truck started to sway and the backend slid, and then the whole truck moved sideways.

"Don't drive like Mom. She's always going too fast then hitting the brakes. Scary as hell."

"Is that how you wrecked your Mustang?" I asked. I couldn't see Joe's face because another corner was coming, and I didn't dare take my eyes off the road. I let my foot off the gas then tapped the brake once. The truck stayed straight, and I found I could use a little gas to finish the curve.

"No, smart guy. That was dry pavement. I was just drunk and going too fast. First time ever." He laughed at his lie.

I shook my head. "I guess we have the right person behind the wheel today then," I said.

The rain had stopped by the time we reached the end of the gravel and turned down a narrow dirt trail barely wide enough for the truck. The trail led away from the road and along a ridge overlooking the Ninilchik River, and we could look into the brushy river bottom and across to the forested slope on the other side. The trail curved away from the river from there and disappeared in the trees, so I stopped the truck.

"This might be a good place to watch for a while," said Joe in a soft voice. We sipped coffee and watched as daylight crept through the trees. Finally, Joe nudged me and said, "You ready? Let's go kill something."

"Born ready," I said.

We left the truck and entered woods along the road and stationed ourselves overlooking the Ninilchik River bottom. I sat for a time on the frame pack to keep my ass off the wet ground and tried to ignore the dampness. A light wind was moving down the river valley, so I pulled up my hood and stuffed my hands in my pockets. I distracted myself by studying the chickadees feeding in the moose brush. They seemed to be in constant motion, the only movement I saw. After nearly an hour, I stood and paced around the tree, swinging my arms to warm up.

The brush along the river was a favored home for moose, and I was surprised that we hadn't seen anything yet. I expected to spot a cow at least. Trails of many passing moose were obvious and fresh droppings lay everywhere. I saw cigarette butts on the ground as I walked back to the truck, reminding me that we weren't the first guys to think this was a good spot to look for moose.

I heard the squeak of brush against rain gear before Joe came into view with rosy cheeks. "Well, what say we call it, Humpy, and head on farther back. I've got my mind set on a lake at the end of this trail that might be the just the spot. Me and Dad took a sixty-incher there five years ago."

"Yeah. I froze my ass off, and you must be a bit sore," I said, noticing the tightness in Joe's face.

He waved it off. "My ass don't like sitting anymore," he said. "Hell of a note."

We walked silently back along the trail to the truck, continuing to hunt with eyes that probed the shadowed forest. Shaggy spruces with wide branches draped to the ground, creating mysterious afternoon shadows. Fresh trails tempted us to walk into the woods, but we stayed on the trail toward the road. Joe wanted to get to the lake and set up camp, but I felt a certain anxiety about getting there in this truck without four-wheel drive. We were crossing the shallow dip across the trail when Joe stopped and pointed. Across the trail from the truck and only a few yards into the forest stood a moose feeding on a willow tree. It was a young cow, but that got our blood up and we were eager to get farther back in the woods.

My worries about how far we could make it out came again a half hour later when we buried the front end of the truck in mud up to the oil pan. Joe was driving this time. He tried shifting into reverse and easing backward out of the hole, but the wheels just spun and threw mud up over the sides of the truck. When that didn't work, he tried giving it the gas, which only sprayed more mud and set us deeper in the hole. "Jesus H. Christ," he growled.

"Well, hell, Joe. Think we're deep enough?" I said without thinking.

"Up yours, smartass!" I flinched, but then he started laughing. "I guess this is as far as we go then," he said. "Looks like a good parking place to me." We climbed out and stood looking up and down the trail, into the mudhole, and under the truck as if some miraculous solution was bound to appear from one of those places.

"Couldn't have done better myself," I said.

"Yup. It takes practice, Humpy. Lots of practice."

"Well, we've seen one moose," I said. "Maybe there's more around here." We were at the base of a low hill with a flat top.

Joe walked up and looked it over. "Good campsite here," he said. "I don't think we would get much farther anyway." He pointed down the trail that led through some black spruce trees onto a muskeg. We could see the water standing in the trail there and the only tracks were from all-terrain track vehicles.

"Yup," I said. "We're as far as the truck will take us, so we might as well camp here."

After we set up the tent, we hunted up and down the trail and then circled back for dinner. That night, we climbed into a cold sleeping bag that smelled of old smoke, mildew, and sweat. The nylon was chilly against my skin so I stayed dressed, removing only my shoes and jacket. While I listened to the wind in the trees and the coyotes announcing the night, on the other side of the tent Joe lay smoking a cigarette. He was just an arm's reach away from me, and I felt the closeness that had started with fried egg sandwiches and had grown through the day. Sleeping on the cold ground had never felt so good.

Joe was already up when I struggled out of my sleeping bag and fumbled in the cold with my stiff boots. Unlike the morning before, there was no stove to stand near and not even a lantern was lit to brighten the gloom of pre-dawn. I stared gloomily at the ground, rubbing a sore spot on my back from sleeping on a root. Then I got up and walked to the edge of camp to stare into the woods and take a leak. Fog as thick as smoke had swallowed the camp, adding to the chill and soaking the tall grass.

Joe seemed comfortable in the cold dark, casually strapping a small bundle to his pack frame. "Here's your breakfast," he said, holding out a piece of jerky and a candy bar. "Let's go kill something."

Ten minutes later, we walked along the trail to the lake, which Joe figured might be another mile farther on. It was a slow march, walking a few yards at a time, then looking and listening, staring into the shadowed brush and across meadows. Our clothes were soon clammy from the fog and wet grass and dripping trees. I flashed back to images from the news of soldiers walking like this, single file with rifles across their bodies, eyes searching as they moved through an Asian forest. I wondered if Joe felt some déjà vu walking like this, hunting.

A wide area opened up before us, and we sat on a fallen log overlooking a muskeg. I wished I'd worn rain pants over my jeans. "Why don't we track them?" I whispered, gesturing toward the distinct hoof prints in the moss.

"Moose sign cuts back and forth through here like a cow pasture," my brother said. "That tells you they're here. You just gotta move slow and keep your eyes and ears open. Once you are in country where moose are, hunting's pretty much just a matter of luck. Maybe you see something, maybe you don't. If you're not lookin', you can walk right past one."

Until this trip, I had thought that all moose crap was the same. "See this?" Joe said, pointing to a pile. "Moose droppings. This is what you look for when you're hunting. Those moose nuggets are old, from last spring, most likely."

"You're kidding! Those are moose droppings?"

"You bet. They eat more green stuff in the summer and their manure is soft because of it. Most of the winter a moose is stuck with willow and birch branches for food, and they pump out those hard little woody nuggets." Joe used a stick to break up a pile and show how the fresh droppings were wet from the rain but dry and brown inside. "If they're fresh, they'll stink and have some fresh green in them."

He looked around. "This is beautiful, isn't it, sitting out in the quiet woods like this, listening to the birds and smelling the changing season?" he said. "This is what Dad loved."

"Yeah, I'm starting to feel it," I said. I had begun to warm and the possibilities of the hunt revived my spirit. Joe surprised me talking like that. I thought it was all about the hunt for Joe.

"Dad used to say the best part of hunting was walking away from camp in the morning and finding a fallen log with a view where he could take a good crap. He's right, you know. There is something about shitting in the woods."

I didn't answer. The moment felt too fragile, and I didn't trust my words. Also, I hadn't taken a crap since we left home and I was long overdue. I stayed quiet while we hunted through the start of morning. Then at nine-thirty, with prime hunting time over, we hunted our way back to camp with our coats tied to our pack. I found myself thinking less about moose and more about breakfast.

Pancakes and dry socks were the highlights of the day, and I watched the sky as the warmth of the sun ate up the fog. After breakfast, we dozed in the grassy hummocks like bears. When I woke, Joe was snoring, so I explored the small hill where we camped.

I was trying to walk the length of a fallen tree when I noticed a strange curl of birch bark nestled in the log's shadow and climbed down to examine it. Someone else had hunted here and left a homemade moose call. Shaped into a cone about a foot long, the glossy bark looked like a megaphone, so I blew into it, experimenting with the sounds I could make. I hooted and booed with the makeshift horn until I recognized sounds like a moose. I'd heard Joe practicing his moose call back at the house. He had a tape of moose calls that he and Frank had spent a whole evening playing. They figured if they could call like moose, they could lure in a big one.

Once I made a sound just like the call of a bull moose on Joe's tape, a moaning guttural bellow that echoed through the spruces and back from across the lake. With each effort, I came closer to repeating the sound that echoed through my head as Joe and Frank had practiced.

Out of breath, I stopped and sat on the log looking guiltily toward the camp, hoping Joe was still napping. Then came a call from the forest, a long-delayed echo of my call coming from the end of the muskeg. I froze and held my breath. That was too long for an echo, and it was different, softer. Ravens skimmed circles overhead while a pair of jays argued in the tree behind me as if all was normal. The call came again. Was it closer? I grabbed the horn and answered. Then I called again. *Nearly perfect*, I thought. Then I ran.

I wanted to shout to Joe, but he was already standing, listening and pointing. When the call came again, Joe grabbed his gun. Then he waited with his gun ready, staring at the small clearing below camp. I grabbed my rifle too, and we stood frozen with our shoulders tight and our heads set at stiff angles. The rifles reached across our heaving chests as if we had already run across the clearing.

The moose appeared from the trees on the other side of the bog. All breathing stopped for a moment. "Son-of-a-bitch! Look at the size of that rack," said Joe. "Come on, buddy. Come to papa."

I squatted in the moss and lifted a pair of binoculars to my eyes. "That's one damn big bull. Did you hear him call, Joe? Did you hear that?"

I was at once stiff and restless, and I felt a tightness in my throat, then the heat and beat of my heart. The moose was right there, an easy kill. Suddenly I wasn't anxious anymore. I wanted to take the shot.

"Shoot," whispered Joe.

Our shots came fast in a thunderous volley. We each fired twice, I think, but the moose just looked across the clearing at the guns and the men standing on the hill. It walked, lifting the long front legs high and forward, breaking into a trot up the steep bank. It fell then, and with our ears ringing from the shooting, we started dancing and patting each other on the back, but it was too soon because the moose was up again and running this time, breaking brush as it crashed through the timber and disappeared.

Joe started swearing. "We had him. Crap! I should have hit him again," he growled.

"He won't go far, taking a hit like that," I said as if I knew what I was talking about.

Joe bent to lace up his boots. "Just relax. We'll get him."

TWENTY-FIVE

A light rain started to fall as we walked across the clearing to where the moose had fallen. We found crushed grass and berry bushes stained with spatters of blood. The blood trail led through shoulder-high ferns and up a hill covered with tall grass overhung with big birch trees. "Nope, he won't get far," said Joe. "Let's spread out along the hill about fifty yards apart. We could walk right past him in this tall grass. And keep that gun ready. Wounded animals are dangerous."

The Model 71 seemed heavy and cumbersome in my hands, like a glove on the wrong hand. I tried to ignore my wet feet and the clammy feel of cooling sweat under my shirt. I forced my legs through wet grass and over fallen logs. We went through dense stands of alders where branches grabbed at gun straps and hats. I felt like the whole hill was fighting against me. Suddenly, I was in a stand of tall alders and I fought through them to a stand of spruce trees with wet moss underfoot. I searched intently until each rotting stump was a moose's back and the golden leaves of the devil's club were antlers. Joe was in my peripheral vision breaking twigs and rattling brush, but neither of us spoke.

Then I no longer heard my brother and the emptiness of the forest surrounded me. Something made me suddenly even more alert, and I crept forward warily. Each sound of a bird or the wind in the trees startled me. The woods darkened, and the powerful firearm in my hand grew heavy. I was hot but still shivering. "At least you're not stuck out here alone for the night," I heard myself say. I tried to clear my mind of apprehension and focus on the moose. My need to find the moose was not like Joe's need. I wasn't just a hunter; this was a quest. The first moose.

Then I saw something to my left—a shape, a movement. It was gone suddenly, and then it was back again, taking form out of the shadows of the forest. Then amid the black and gray, the form of a man, and I realized that Joe had gotten a little ahead of me. I turned the rifle away before he saw me.

Then I spied something else. Nearly hidden by a fallen birch log was a mound of hair and antlers. Then the head became clear and looked at me—a single black eye. Raising my rifle ready to shoot, I peered through the sights down the barrel. My heart raced as the moment became huge. This was my time. Then Joe was there again in my sights with his dark raincoat, cap, and pack all in focus at the end of my barrel, my finger on the trigger. I gasped and nearly dropped my rifle.

"Shit. That was close," I murmured. Joe moved out of my view. And the moose that was clear in my eyes was now the roots of a fallen spruce and the stump of a birch tree. No moose at all.

TWENTY-SIX

I woke to the clatter of pots and pans outside the tent. My first thought was a bear, but I was unsure even where I was. My head was confusing the dreams of the night and the reality of the day before. I remembered hunting, but I was hunting in my dreams too. I couldn't figure out which was real, the one I had just left in sleep or yesterday's hunt. Both were vivid, in some ways perfect, but in my dream I was the hunter, the shooter, the moose killer.

Like all dreams, this hunting had taken place in a twisted setting with pieces from my life tangled up in it. Iris was hunting with me in the woods behind the high school. There were wolves there with blood on their muzzles, and then they left. Iris left too, so I started hunting her, stalking through the mixed-up dream forest, looking for the girl instead of the moose. Suddenly Joe was there too, and I shot the moose while Iris laughed at me with the wolves watching. I knew they were jealous of me and my rifle and the girl. The wolves ran off when the pans rattled.

I came out of the tent and found Joe pouring coffee from a thermos he'd loaded the night before. He offered it to me without speaking. I could still feel the damp but didn't mind as much this morning. "You look cold," Joe said. He handed me a down vest. I put it on over my sweatshirt even though it smelled like an old duffel bag.

"Thanks," I said and put on my raincoat and grabbed my knapsack and rifle. The images from the hunt were strong in me now, and I was confident about finding our moose or another for me to shoot today. Yesterday we had run out of light before we found the wounded one, but as Joe said, "Tomorrow's another day."

With hunting lust in me, I followed Joe eagerly as we took the trail around a small lake and worked our way through the brush and up to the ridge we followed the day before. From the ridge, we spread out and walked straight down and across muskeg before entering the forest again.

We spent two hours poking into soggy bogs and meadows of grass standing over my head. The area was crisscrossed with moose sign. We would walk a few steps and then stop to peer into the shadows of the trees or through the open clearings hoping for another moose. Following Joe's lead, we hunted an arc around to the north and back to camp for a midday nap and lunch. By that time, the thrill of yesterday's success had worn off and Joe was quiet and grumpy, squatting in the truck cab to eat Vienna sausages and beans.

The rain stopped late in the day and then we went hunting again, this time walking east out of camp away from the trail. "I'd like to check that old burn about a mile up from the lake," said Joe. "It might turn up somethin'."

"Sounds good as anything," I said with enthusiasm. "Don't need any more of that rain."

Joe grabbed his rifle and pulled his hat down tight on his head. "Saddle up, cowboy," he said. "And don't forget: if we get split up, remember the signal Dad and me always used. One lone shot means nothing. Only when it's followed by two more shots five minutes later with a count of ten between would you know a moose is down."

"Okay, Joe. Let's get this big fella."

We hunted, spreading out fifty yards apart, until we reached an area burned by wildfire. The trees were just black poles standing in a field of charred moss. Here and there among the trees were clumps of willow brush and young birches not much taller than us, but most everything was burned black or covered with gray ash. I couldn't keep from shivering when I looked into the cold heart of the blackened forest. I knew from science class that forest fires cleared the forest so that new browse grew for moose, and the clumps of willow and young birch would be attractive feed for them. But for me, it seemed dead, dark, and threatening.

We perched on blowdowns a hundred yards apart to peer into the acres of naked tree trunks. We sat for about an hour and ate sticks of smoked salmon as we watched and cursed the damp weather. The rain started again, and finally Joe waved me in to stand under a tree out of the rain.

"We need to spread out," he said, looking hopefully into the woods. "I'd like to follow the edge of this burn a ways."

"Sounds good to me," I said. "I'll work along this edge to that far ridge and then turn around. This trail runs right along to the lake, right? And at the north end of the lake, there's a bog and creek before I get to camp."

Joe sank down on a log and put his head against the barrel of his rifle. "I'm glad you've been paying attention, Humpy. I'd hate to lose you out here."

I could feel the confidence strong in me now and it was driving me forward. Before, I had been nervous when Joe was even out of sight. But now was my chance. "Don't get your shorts into a knot, Joe. I got this."

"Reckon we gotta do something to change our luck," he said. "But we got to do something now, or we are going to run out of daylight. We've got a couple of hours of good hunting time left."

Joe stood up, broad and dark in his dark-green rain gear. "Now, Sam, listen to me. You stay on this line along the burn and work your way slowly along it for an hour, then turn around and follow it back." He tied a strip of plastic ribbon to a spruce bow and pointed west toward the lake. I tried not to show my excitement. I knew so perfectly now that the moose would be mine.

"You got your watch?"

I nodded.

"We'll meet back here at seven. This flag will show you where to turn toward the lake. And remember, there are grassy little meadows in this burn and a moose could be lying down in any one of those. And you hunt with your ears—listen, Humpy, listen." I nodded again. "Any time you can climb up on a log or stump, do it. Moose can be hard to spot, so move slowly and keep an eye out." I could tell Joe was more nervous than I was about splitting up. He couldn't see me as I was yet. The moose would change that.

"Got it," I said.

With a final wave, Joe turned and took the twenty steps necessary to disappear from view. I was alone in the forest. The moose was out there, and I would find it and kill it. This day was mine. The same energy that burned through me before the peace march and the same confidence I felt when I toed the line with Phelps was boosting my spirits and inspiring me. I began to move down the edge of the burn with a confidence I'd not found outside of Pete's kitchen. I would take my first moose. Everything else was in the past. I thought only of the hunt. This was a whole new level for me.

I moved silently and slowly, peering down into the woods and the small grassy clearings in the burn. Last week's frost had turned the birch leaves golden, and the edges of the alders were tinged with brown as if scorched over the campfire. On my right, the blackened trunks poked toward the sky or lay scattered like pickup sticks. The high-bush cranberries leaves were bright red now, and the overripe berries gave off an odor like dirty socks.

When it was time to turn around, I paused and looked back the way I came. I removed my coat and wadded it to fit in my rucksack. When a particularly inviting opening in the trees presented itself, I walked away from the burn and the lake and from camp into the untracked forest. The moose was still before me, and I wasn't ready to quit. *Just a little farther,* I told myself, *just a few more minutes.*

Suddenly I saw movement across a bog, and I froze mid-stride. I stood in one place listening to the pounding of my heart as my eyes prepared to see the trophy appear, and I scanned the shadows beneath the spruces.

When no animal showed itself, I walked out into the bog until I felt the water begin to soak into my shoes. With each step, the surface became softer and wetter, and the thick moss bounced beneath my feet as if it were floating on the body of water that formed the small pond in the center of the bog. I turned back, but then the moss gave way completely and one leg sank up to the hip.

"Oh, oh, *oh!*" I yelped as the cold water rushed around my leg, and I fell facedown in the wet sphagnum. At first I was just shocked at the bitingly cold water, then I was pissed at the soaking I was getting as water came through the cuffs of the rain pants. The moss was like a soggy sponge floating in a pan of dirty dishwater, and when I pushed down on it to try to rise, my hands sank into it, taking my head and shoulders with it. I reared up thrashing. "Oh shit!" I had never learned to swim and now I was in a pool of water that seemed bottomless. I panicked, flailed around wildly with my arms, gasping for breath.

I called without realizing it. "Help! Help me!" My voice echoed in trees. No answer came. My legs sank as the spongy raft began to slip lower in the water. I threw the rifle ahead of me toward firmer ground. The thrust of that motion threw me sideways onto my back, and I could feel my knapsack pulling me down further and my head felt the icy grip of terror. I rolled back to my belly and sank even more then floated up.

I wasn't just cold and wet, I was fighting for my life. I fought the water and the moss and the fear surging through me. This wasn't in the dream, but I wish it had been. Then it wouldn't be real. An icy fever burned through my muscles, and I fought to control it. I couldn't stop thrashing though, and I could hear my great moaning gasp as I fought for a way out. The safety of the firm ground was only a couple of feet away, but it might as well have been a mile. The water was rising around my body, and every move I made just let my soggy moss raft undulate so that water washed into my clothes and the chill deepened.

Inside a voice told me, *Lie still. You'll float.* But I ignored it and fought harder against water and the floating sphagnum moss. Then I lunged and kicked until I found myself across the water-soaked moss, away from the icy pond that pulled at my clothes. I grabbed at small bushes that had their roots in solid ground. They held, and I kept grabbing and wriggling forward on my belly until my chest felt the firmness of the earth beneath me where the moss again supported my weight. I rolled and kicked my way free of the water and the moss and the terror.

Water was under my rain pants, pooling around my soggy shirt and chilling me from head to foot. I crawled on my belly to the rifle and then threw it again. I crawled closer, but the knapsack was a soggy weight flopping around on my back so I rolled out of the shoulder straps. Then I crawled up to the base of a birch where I clung to its stable, solid roots.

I was cold to the bone in wet clothes, and the dream of finding the moose began to fade. I had hunted the ridge and there was no moose for me there. I was shivering, wet, and alone. I forgot how much Joe had scared me a few nights ago at the Inlet View Cafe, and now I wanted him here. If Joe were here, I would feel safe and strong. But he wasn't, and I didn't feel safe at all.

I removed my boots and poured out the water. Then I peeled the socks from my clammy white feet and wrung them out. "No sense carrying extra water," I muttered. I tried to squeeze water from the ends of my pant legs and shirt too. My hands were shaking, and not just from the cold. I jammed my feet back into wet socks and boots, tucked in my shirts, and tightly buttoned the wool jacket up to my chin. I pulled my raincoat over the still damp clothes and found a wool cap in my knapsack, along with some brown jersey gloves for my stiff, red hands.

With my bandana, I wiped the Model 71 clean of dirt and clinging spruce needles, and checked the bore to make sure that nothing clogged it. I ran my hand over the smooth stock and the cold smooth steel of the barrel as if I could feel the power within.

That's when I heard the shot.

TWENTY-SEVEN

It was one rifle shot, a roaring blast through the trees that shook me out of my daze. Before the echo faded from the silent forest, I was up and moving, rifle in hand, head clear. Joe, somewhere near, had fired at something. Forgetting my wet clothes and soggy feet, I ran through the brush toward the sound. It was like I had been summoned, as if I only had to cross the street to be there with Joe. I would be there to share the moment of success. I would be there to see the last twitching death throes of the animal that I should have killed.

This is wrong, I thought. I should have fired that shot. I should be standing over the dead moose. But instead I was running through the woods, wet and lost like a stupid kid. I *was* lost, and I had lost the moose. I'd lost the sun too, and thick, threatening clouds were gathering above me.

I had been running for several minutes, but now, with no sound to guide me, I had nowhere to go. The edge of the burn was not a straight line. The fire had reached fingers of flame into the forest, and there were even small circles of burned trees in the middle of the untouched live ones. In other places, the fire had burned around parts of the forest, leaving lush islands in its blackened swath.

The cold and fear that panicked me at the bog returned, and the trees began to spin in my vision. I sat down and stared dully at the ground, my breathing growing heavier until I was panting like a dog. My attention was torn between the fear of being lost and the disappointment of not finding the moose. The moose was supposed to have been mine, but with one shot the chance of that was gone. Joe must have found him, and I had lost my orientation to the lake and the ridge. Like the dream, my hope began to fade. "Goddamnit! Son-of-a-bitch!" I yelled, but only the wet world around me could hear.

The outburst seemed to clear my mind, and I remembered something. There had been no two shots. Has it been five minutes? I hadn't checked my watch, but I smiled. Joe may have shot and missed, maybe even missed a different moose that wasn't his bull. The hunt was still on then and the opportunity still existed for me to make the kill that I knew was mine. No matter how many times a hunter shot at a moose, he was supposed to wait five minutes then fire two more if the kill had been made. That was the signal to come and share in the butchering. I sat on the ground drinking the last of my water, looking at my watch.

I forced myself to concentrate and study my surroundings. To my left, the grove of birches rose to a ridge and mixed their straight, shiny trunks with the sprawling branches of the spruce. The ridge continued around in an arch to enclose a grassy meadow. Between it and me was a fringe of muskeg. A well-used game trail led toward the meadow, so I followed it to the edge where I found a pile of fresh moose droppings. Unlike the classic winter nuggets that are shaped like giant brown jellybeans, these were glossy, soft globs that stuck together in a pile that steamed when I pushed it apart with my shoe. Fresh sign!

Now my senses were all lit up. I stared into my surroundings, pushing my view deeper into the alder patch. I had found a fresh trail and the surroundings looked familiar. A moose, maybe a big bull, had passed here today. I blew a long, slow, quiet breath. Perhaps my moment was at hand.

The gun was heavy and strong in my hand as I pushed the barrel through the low opening between the first of the alders and followed the trail forward. Large, deep tracks were stamped in the bed of forest, and I fought the urge to hurry my steps. The moose was near.

I was cold and wet and hungry, but I pushed those feelings aside to focus. I crossed the meadow and climbed over the low ridge beyond it. Then I dropped down toward another muskeg with a pond in the center. That's when I heard the second shot, closer this time.

I charged down the ridge toward the pond. In the shadow of the spruce bows where the forest was thick, I caught a movement then the contrast of white against black. Antlers! Moose antlers were making small motions of light in a dusk-veiled forest. Safety off. The ears appeared then the whole head. Stop panting. Don't shake. The dream was real. This was no trick of light like yesterday. This moose was real.

Beneath the antlers was the head, beneath the head the neck—invisible but there—and behind the neck, the shoulder. Squeeze, don't jerk. Breath out. Fire. A flash from the muzzle, the roar. Falling antlers dropping in the shadows. The cry. A scream. Then silence.

As soon as I fired the rifle, the image came into focus. *Joe!* Joe was lifting the moose's head, turning the antlers to set them square. Joe was there in the shot with the moose when the bullet left the chamber of my gun. Joe was the motion I saw. The single shot from my Model 71 Winchester crossed a small clearing where the two-hundred-fifty grain bullet found its mark.

I did not move. My arms fell to my sides and the rifle dropped from my hand. A cold chill of fear blew down my back like the cold water from the pond, and the trees rushed around me. I managed two steps forward. "Joe! Joe!" I had to see. I couldn't see. It was all beyond me. The bullet could not be called back. I ran toward Joe, into the falling rain with the cold wind of death at my back. I only ran a couple of steps before I tripped and fell. I scrambled up and saw the light hitting off the antler of the moose pointing skyward against the rain that fell into this forest.

I rose against the rain and the fear and followed the path of the bullet, my bullet, following it across the opening between the spruces dripping the rain onto the scene of my irrevocable action. Joe wasn't moving. I wanted to rush forward and grab him, but my feet slowed and I walked forward slowly as if approaching a casket.

Joe had hit the ground with one antler lying across his chest. His eyes were wide, filled with surprise and questions, but after his original yell, he was silent. His mouth gasped desperately for air. The bubbles of blood came out his nose and a bloody stream ran down his cheek. The side of his head was black with blood. He closed his eyes and opened them and stared. A gust of wind blew through the treetops, rattling the dying birch leaves.

This time when I ran, I ran away. I ran until I could run no more. I ran until the tripping and falling wore me down, and I was left leaning against a tree, gasping for breath.

I slumped to the ground, each detail replaying itself in my mind in an endless loop. The gloomy dusk of a cloudy fall day, the sound of rain drizzling in the trees, the faint outline against the forest silhouette, antlers boldly white in the gray mist. They were all there and moving—and I fired. I fired and the bullet hit Joe. How could I go forward? How could I face Mom and tell her I had killed my only brother? *He's a killer*, people would say. *That poor family.*

"My God! I killed my brother." I said it aloud, trying to make it just a nightmare, but it was real, and I was bombarded by images, by the terror. Somewhere behind me, Joe lay on his back, mouth open and bleeding, staring at eternity.

Every step, every detail kept replaying as I gasped for air and clenched my eyes closed, trying to shut out the world around me. I felt a pounding in my gut and then a spasm of my diaphragm and my mouth opened wide. I vomited into the moss once, twice, then gagged without vomiting while chills ran through me. On my knees, I cried and shivered, hugging myself against the pain of reality.

Slowly, I calmed and the breathing slowed, the warmth began to return, and I opened my eyes. The choice was suddenly clear. I could never go back. I rose and walked into a dense stand of trees, the darkest part of the woods. Here, the trees were small and close together. Some only twice as tall as me but so tightly packed together that I could barely walk between them. I felt as if I were a mouse in the grass. The sweat that soaked my clothes began to cool and the chill from my dunking returned. The gray sky pressed down on me like the clouds were stone and the rain was rocks falling on me.

I fell, and instead of rising, I pressed my face into the soggy cold moss. I cried a bit, then I lay still. I was ready to give up then. But I couldn't stop listening. The *drip, drip, drip* of rain tumbling through the spruce boughs made a steady rattle all around me. Then a little breeze pushed one set of branches, and its falling water startled me. My heart slowed, my hands quit shaking, and I knew immediately that I was in the wrong place. I couldn't just give up here. Maybe Joe wasn't dead. Scared, wet, and cold like me, but not dead. And I wasn't dead either. If I was alive, there was a chance for Joe.

Another wave of guilt struck. If I died here alone in this wet forest of black spruce, it meant Joe would die too, if he hadn't already. I couldn't let Joe die. I didn't want to die either—not really. With all the bad that I had done, I still wasn't strong enough to want death.

TWENTY-EIGHT

"Frank?" Joe's voice was weak, barely audible. He lay with half his body under the moose's head and his face cut and bloody. The broad paddle of one antler lay on his chest, pressing against his ribs. I had found Joe at the edge of night, at the edge of death, and I knew right then he'd rather Frank was there than me.

"No, it's me. Sam. I'm here." I leaned close with one hand on the moose's head. "I'm here, Joe."

"Sam."

"Yeah, it's me," I said. I wanted to move him out from under the weight of all that antler and head, but I was shaking and weak, uncertain. Blood clung to my hand when I touched him and I drew back, away from the clammy feel of it.

"Frank?"

"He's back home, Joe. Remember?" I knew I should be doing something, but all I could think at that moment was to stare at Joe, helpless.

"Sorry, Sam."

I started to choke up. "No! I'm sorry. I'm worse than sorry . . ."

"It's okay. Lost, Sam . . . Don't get lost on me. We're in the shit now."

When he said that, it jolted me. I pressed a trembling hand on Joe's shoulder, examining the wound as I listened, but it was too dark to see anything. I was *in the shit.* "Don't worry, Joe."

"Sam . . . you . . . ya shot me?"

"Yes." The words made me writhe. "It was all my fault, Joe. I didn't think."

" 's okay."

"Yeah, well . . . I'm gonna fix you up," I said grimly, fighting to control the sobs, the grief, the fear. "You just lie there and wait for the sun to come up." I could feel the hole in the slicker and the blood around it, and more blood was leaking through a gash across the shirt front. I reached a hand down along Joe's back and felt the softness of flesh and the open wound. My trembling hand dragged through the blood-soaked moss beneath him. I couldn't believe I wasn't vomiting. I longed for the sun.

"Flashlight," Joe said.

I dug in his pocket and found it. "Got it." Suddenly the man lay in a circle of light. Too much light now. I could see the deathlike face smeared with blood and crushed leaves. I could see the ripped shirt and torn muscle lying open to the night. I could see blood by his leg. My stomach came up to my throat. I thought I was going to lose it again, but I turned and grabbed the canteen instead.

I grabbed the antlers and lifted. The moose's head came up and I pulled it off Joe. The head tried to fall back onto him, but with a final strain I turned it enough to be resting on one antler instead of Joe's chest. I pulled him away just a bit and put the canteen to his lips and he sipped some water. From my pack, I pulled out a first aid kit and opened it on my lap. Darkness made it hard to see, even with the flashlight, but I could tell that the kit only had some Band-Aids and little packets of aspirin. I heard myself jabbering. "I guess this isn't much of a first aid kit, is it? Next time we better bring a better one. 'Course then we won't need it. That's why we carry emergency gear, right?" My hands and voice were shaking. "So we won't need it."

The bullet had cut a furrow across Joe's chest, and his face and neck were cut. I couldn't tell how bad. When I folded down the bib on his rain pants back for a better look, Joe moaned and then I saw where the bullet had torn into the right leg above the knee as well.

I had nothing in my kit big enough for a bandage, so I dug in Joe's pack that lay on the ground beside the moose carcass. Even as I worked, I felt the panic lingering at the edge of my consciousness, a coyote waiting to take what I left. A black snarl of dread was at my elbow the whole time.

A cotton game bag was stuffed at the bottom of Joe's pack. It was like a pillowcase big enough to hold a moose quarter. "We've got some bandages here after all, Joe." He groaned as I cut away his shirt and spread the bag across his chest. The wound on the leg was more sensitive than the chest, and I thought I saw bits of bone sticking out of it. That made me queasy, but I pushed through the nausea.

Joe looked up at me with eyes suddenly clear. "Splint the leg," he said. "Wrap the chest. Do it right."

"Okay, Joe. I'm on it." I bit my lip so he wouldn't hear the terror in me and see how close I was to losing it. I covered the leg wound with a clean handkerchief that I found in the pack, mostly so I didn't have to look at it.

I paused and thought about Joe's instructions. Yes, the leg needed a splint to keep the broken bone stable and I'd seen enough Western movies to know what it should look like. Another time I would have made a joke about the John Wayne school of first aid.

"A splint for the leg, then I gotta wrap that chest wound," I said. I needed to tear that cotton game bag and wrap his chest. "First the splint, Sam," I said to myself. I took Joe's Kabar knife from the sheath on his belt and continued to talk aloud as I cut tree limbs for splints and then dug up a parachute cord from my rucksack. "Okay, Joe. Here we go. This might hurt, I bet." I lay the splints on either side of his thigh then lifted his leg to start wrapping the parachute cord.

He didn't yell like I would have. He was panting hard though, fighting the urge to scream into the night. "Tighter!" Joe growled through clenched teeth. I tightened it. I knew it had to be done. I had to keep hurting him. There was no easy way.

With the splint in place, I let him rest while I folded a long john shirt into a pad for his chest. "Sorry," I murmured. "Must hurt terrible, huh. I-I don't know what to do."

"Get Frank."

I stared glumly at the forest fringe and wished I could. God, I wished I could. I wished I could call in a medic like a soldier would, but there was only me and the darkness with the dead moose and the wounded brother and the rain. I shook my head and went back to work. I put the folded shirt on the wound and ripped the game bag down the middle. I remembered Mom bandaging a cut finger with a strip torn from her hankie. She wrapped the strip around the finger a couple of times, then spit the end of the bandage to make two ties that held it in place. I could do that with the game bag, but I'd have to get Joe sitting up with his rain gear off.

"Joe. This is going to hurt some more," I said. "I have to get you in a sitting position. And cut off your raincoat." He nodded his head. "On a count of three, I'm going to sit you up. Then I'll take off your raincoat and wrap your chest. Got it?"

"Let's get this shit over with."

Joe's eyes rolled back in his head, and I looked away and started my count. "One, two . . ." On three I lifted him, and he screamed then sat there panting.

I wrapped the strips of cotton around his chest with the rain coming down on us. He was cold and pale, shivering. He looked like death. "My ribs," he moaned. I was doing what I had to do, but it might not be enough.

Joe passed out then. I caught him and eased him back down on his raincoat and took off mine and covered him with it. I was cold too and thought about a fire. I walked out from the moose kill to a dead sapling. I bent it until it snapped at the roots and came out into my hands, then I dragged it over and leaned it on the dead moose and went back for more. When I had a dozen small dead trees, I broke limbs and made a small pile. They were dry on the inside, but the outsides were soaked. Everything was wet.

"Fire. You makin' fire?" Joe muttered. I dropped my sticks and went to Joe, leaning close. "Birch bark and dead branches . . ." He paused and breathed. "Like I taught you. Got your matches? Branches . . . kindling from the bottom of the spruce. Remember?"

"Yeah, Joe, I remember." I grabbed a flashlight and went into the trees. The low branches seemed to grab at me, trying to draw me back into the forest and the panic, but I fought it away from the front of me. I had a fire to build.

All the campfires I'd built with Joe to roast wieners or marshmallows helped ready me for this. I built a base with five sticks about the size of my arm. On this platform I cross-stacked smaller branches the size of a finger, but I had no birch bark to stuff in the center for tinder.

I looked around frustrated as I pulled the shotgun shell from my pocket, the one Joe gave me that was full of matches, then I felt for the other shell I found from the cabin on the bluff. I still had it too. With my knife I cut through the plastic casing and let the pellets fall out on the ground. A plastic plug lay under them and I pried it out and poured the gunpowder on the damp sticks. I struck a match and touched it to the gunpowder. It flashed bright with an eruption of orange, and then the kindling caught. The branches from the spruce caught easily too, and slowly the glow of a campfire filled the night with light. Just the sight of it nurtured my hope. I fed the fire more wood, hungry for its heat and light.

I wanted to build two more fires to make a triangle around the Joe, a triangle of warmth and light to push back the night and to be a beacon. Maybe it was stupid to think a plane would fly by, but signal fires were part of my new hope. For the first time since I pulled the trigger, I could see a way out.

Joe was sleeping but woke suddenly. "Saw one," he said.

I stopped feeding the fire and bent closer. "What?"

"Meteor, Frank. I saw one. Going to take me home. I bet when I go my spirit will take off like that, a streak of light across the sky." I wondered what he saw in the cloud-covered sky, and it scared me.

"No. You can't!" I knelt and clutched his hand. The hand was cold, even colder than me, and that shook me. I couldn't move him closer to the fire and he wasn't getting any heat from it. "You're cold, huh, Joe. Me too, but stay with me, brother." I looked up, hoping someone would suddenly appear out of the forest and help me. A foolish, childish hope, to think there was anyone within miles of us. I turned back to the moose and ran a hand over the brown hide. The odor was strong and the heat of the animal was still in it. "The hide! Gonna get you a good moose hide cover, Joe!"

I pulled my hunting knife from my belt. It was smaller than Joe's Kabar, but sharp and light for skinning. I jabbed it into the moose between the back legs by the ball sack. I had never butchered an animal alone before, but I'd been there when Dad butchered one. "I can do this," I said. I had to open the skin along the belly without puncturing the stomach, but I had to work fast, so I just kept cutting in the fickle dancing light of the campfire.

I cut up to the rib cage and the stomach bulged out, pressing against the membrane like a giant balloon. I cut straight up to the neck, then up each front leg and around the hoof. I skinned each leg by pulling the hide out from the meat and running the knife along the meat to separate the hide. Finally, I ran the knife along the spine and pulled half of the hide free of the carcass. I hadn't punctured the membrane that held the guts inside the moose, so it lay like a great pink balloon exposed to the sky, the red meat of the legs shining in the firelight.

I spread the hide on the ground beside Joe. "Gotta move you onto this hide, Joe. Let's get you out of the wet."

"I'm done in, Frank. I know you're just here keepin' watch, waiting for a chopper, waiting for a body bag. Never leave a man behind, right, buddy?"

"I'm Sam, Joe. Frank's not here." I wondered why that son-of-a-bitch Frank kept coming to mind. "I got you, brother. I got you." Did he think I couldn't save him? Yeah, maybe Frank knew all that first aid stuff, but he wasn't here. I was here. I could save my brother.

I put my mind back on getting Joe out of the wet moss and onto the moose hide. I couldn't lift the man, so I rolled him. Joe landed on his side, yelled, "*Ahh!*" then shivered and passed out.

"Yeah, Sam's here, Joe. I got you." I leaned over him. "Joe, stay with me." But the face showed no response. He was still breathing though, so I spread my raincoat over him and wrapped the moose hide over and around him. The hide still held the heat of the moose, and I hoped some of the warmth was reaching him.

Between trips to collect fuel for the other fires, I cut green boughs to keep some of the rain off Joe. I tried to roll the moose over, but even with the leverage of the long legs, I couldn't. "Gotta be a way, Sam," I said, thinking out loud again. "Maybe if you gut the moose. Yeah, gut the damn moose, dumbass."

Tied to Joe's pack was about twenty feet of quarter-inch rope. I knotted the rope to a rear hoof of the moose, then stretched it out to a spruce tree and tied it so that the moose was spread-eagled. Then I used my knife to open the belly and rolled the guts out on the ground. By the time the steaming gut pile was out and away from the moose, I was panting and sweating, covered in blood from my nose to my knees, and feeling strong again.

I wanted to roll the moose over to get to the other half of the hide. "Keep going, Sam," I chanted, "keep going. Roll the moose. Strip the hide. Keep going, Sam." I grabbed a leg and tried rolling the carcass, but the head and antlers fought against me so I had to roll them first. When I grabbed the antlers, I felt a stabbing pain in my hand. I put the flashlight beam on it and found a splinter from the antler imbedded in my palm. My bullet must have broken the antler before hitting Joe, and the splinters of antler had cut his face and neck. The jagged edge had stabbed his chest, and the bullet might still be in his leg, but getting it out wasn't something I was ready to do. I pulled the splinter from my hand with my teeth, and my blood mixed with Joes on my hand.

With the moose head turned the other way and the rope on the hind leg pulled tight, I was able to put all my strength on one front leg and roll the moose onto its skinned side. I took a break to check on Joe and feed the fire. Come daylight, I would throw on green boughs to make smoke. The fire marked the forest with dancing ghosts, but the low overcast shrouded the clearing from above. Only high-flying jets would be out in this weather anyway. Joe lay still and silent on his moose-hide bed. His wounds still wept blood, but only slightly. He drank the water I offered, but that was all. No words, no movement.

After skinning the other half of the moose and covering Joe with it, I moved closer to the fire and removed the wet down vest Joe had given me earlier in the day before I knew what cold really was. The vest was now soggy and clinging to the long johns beneath it. The steam rose from it as I held it out to the heat. The fire warmed me and I wanted food—not candy bars but real, hearty food.

I looked desperately through my pack and then my eyes fell on the moose. “Sam, you idiot,” I said, “there’s a whole pile of food sitting in front of you.” In minutes, I had strips of moose meat sizzling on a stick by the fire. When the meat was brown and starting to drip fat, I cut it in tiny pieces and carried them on a piece of birch bark to Joe. He refused the meat but drank more water. I ate the pieces I’d cut, then went back to the fire and ate more of the charred meat.

If only there was a radio, some way to call for help. I thought about the truck and our camp. I had to get Joe there. Then I had to get help or get the truck unstuck. My breath came fast and I felt my heart racing again. I couldn’t do all this. “Shit, shit, shit. Oh, what a goddamn mess.”

Joe started muttering, “No, Frank, he didn’t mean it. I’m done.”

I turned and listened.

“Like in the movies.” Joe coughed heavily. “Used up,” he said.

I kneeled beside him, feeling helpless. “I’m doing everything I can for you, Joe. Don’t you give up on me!”

“Go.” His voice showed his weakness. “Go find Frank. Go home. Go, Sam.”

I buried my face in the wet slicker. I knew Joe was worried about me instead of himself, but worry wasn’t what I needed. I needed help—food and shelter and help—and I hated myself for wanting all of that. The only help I got was a break in the rain.

It made sense that Joe would want his friend there to help him. Someone he’d been *in the shit* with instead of me. But I was here, and the anger and frustration of what happened before had been left behind. It didn’t matter anymore how mad I was about Joe and the war. All that had been forgotten now.

I shivered in a fever of confusion. Then slowly, like a filling tub, warmth spread through me and I saw beyond this makeshift camp in the woods. If Joe was gone, if he died, I could not imagine returning. How could people, especially Mom, forgive such a deed?

And then I was home, knocking on the door. She came to the doorway to welcome me and looked past me for Joe. She kept looking and looking until she knew, and then she closed the door with me on the front step, alone before a closed door. Joe was the one she would be looking for. Joe, the wounded soldier. Joe, who came home from the war when she was sure he wouldn't. Joe, who did the stuff Dad used to do now that Dad couldn't. I was just Sam. Sam skipped school and broke curfew. Sam left chores undone and rebelled against the family. Sam was always sorry. She wouldn't be looking for Sam now.

I saw her in the wingback chair in the front room of that log cabin where Dad died, her face old and red.

"What am I supposed to do now?" she asked. "What can you do to make up for this? You have no idea what it's like to live with such loss. How much am I supposed to bear?"

"Mom," I tried. "Mom, I didn't mean to. I was . . ."

"You never mean to. You never mean to do one damn thing, but you do, don't you? Am I that bad of a mother?"

"Mom, no. I'm sorry."

I let the cold creep up my legs like a thousand spiders as the wet socks and pants sucked out the warmth the fire and movement had given. I felt myself slipping. I was relaxing now that I was with Joe and Joe was alive. Before, I had been so close to the end, and I was sure Joe was gone, but now in the black rain of night, I was weak again, unable to see how to make it past this moment. I could easily give up now. The pain in my heart receded into a gathering blackness.

TWENTY-NINE

I woke up cold—desperate, trembling cold. But through that cold, I heard spruce wood crackling in a fire and I breathed the smoke of a campfire. Was this a dream? No, the smoke was real, and I was at the kill site, at the scene of the crime, and I still breathed. I hadn't slept long. I could tell from the fire still burning energetically.

Then I heard Joe. "Stay down! Stay down!" He was yelling, but his voice was weak, almost a whisper. I scrambled up and went to him. His head rocked back and forth with his eyes crushed closed. "Wait for mortar cover!" His arms fought the heavy moose hide that covered him. "Call it in! Hold! Hold!" He mumbled more words, words I couldn't understand, but I knew he wasn't with me. He was back in Vietnam, back *in the shit*, back to a place I had taken him.

He opened his eyes suddenly, and when I put my hand on his shoulder, he blinked then smiled. "Sam. Good job." Then he closed his eyes again, but I heard his breathing slow and he was quiet. I stoked the fire and hovered over Joe, unsure about the next move.

"Hang the meat," Joe said.

I leaned closer. "What?"

"Hang the meat." He took a deep breath and winced when he did. "Can't waste it. Hang the meat. It'll rot." He was back now, awake.

"I'll get you some water," I said, looking at the skinned carcass of the moose as I found the canteen I had carried. I knew what he had in mind. Left on the ground, the meat would stay wet and warm. It would rot quickly. If I was going to save it, I'd need to mount a pole between two trees, cut the moose into four to six pieces, and hang them on the pole.

I gave him sips of water from his canteen, but it splashed down in front. It was an Army surplus canteen with a canvas case and a big cup that it nested in. I poured water into the cup, and he sipped from it steadily.

"Joe, we gotta get you out first. Then I'll come back for the meat. I don't have enough line to do all that tying." I wasn't sure I had the strength left for the job either, but I wouldn't admit that.

Joe rolled to his good side. "No, let me rest. I'm not bleeding bad. You cook us some meat. Build a rack. I'll supervise." But I could tell that hurt, and he lay back down on his back.

"All right, Joe. Just rest." I knew he was right. We should save the meat if we could, and a little rest before trying to drag him out of here might be good. I thought maybe some broth would go down better than just meat, so I filled his canteen cup with meat and water and then set it at the edge of the fire.

By the time I found a spruce sapling to use for a meat pole, a hint of light was showing above the trees, and I knew the night was almost over. I had gone the whole night with almost no sleep and without being afraid of the darkness. I was alone in the dark woods with only my wounded brother, but I had gotten past the fear of it. I sat on a corner of the moose hide beside my brother and looked into the fire, into the distance where I saw Iris sitting by another fire with another guy, a guy who kept his cool and made the right choices. The peace symbol I wore felt cold inside my shirt, like an ice cube against my skin. I decided then that maybe I'd give her a call when we got home. It was worth a try... if we ever got home.

My day's work was before me. I needed to act, to move, to fight death as best I could. There was nothing else but the here and now. There was only me, and I had a moose to butcher and hang.

Neither of us was carrying a hatchet, so I used Joe's heavy Kabar knife to cut the branches from the sapling, then looked around for a pair of trees to hang it in. I found a pair of spruces about seven feet apart that had branches coming out at about the same level. I lifted the pole and seated it about a foot above my head. The next step was to get the meat up there. Not a hard job if I had help, but I didn't. That was nobody's fault but mine. I stopped and looked at the knife in my hand and wondered what places it had been, what cuts it had made. I remembered it stuck in the bar at the Inlet View with Roger Miller singing in the background. I was cold again for a moment, but I was humming that song. *Dang me, dang me.*

I gave Joe more water and set his broth away from the fire to cool. Then I cut some strips of meat and put them on green sticks to cook. The Kabar made easy work of cutting the legs and shoulders off the moose. I decided to leave the rib cage and spine since they didn't have much meat. I went back to Joe's moose and cut strips of hide to use for hanging the meat.

Without pause, I bent and lifted a leg of moose to hang on the pole and continued that work until all four legs and the meaty backbone hung in the morning air. Each piece was heavy, likely the most weight I'd ever lifted. I cut green boughs and shingled them on the pole over the meat to protect it from birds and rain. It was the best I could do.

"You ate some of the moose?"

I sat beside Joe chewing a strip of charred backstrap still hot and dripping juice. "Yeah, I did. And I made you some soup." I raised the canteen cup.

Joe nodded. I held the cup so he could sip, but that didn't work so I propped him up to a half-sitting position. He started slow but kept sipping at the broth. “Needs salt,” he said. Then he smiled.

“Yup, I’ll tell the chef,” I said. I chewed my steak. Then I lay him back and covered him again. In the pale light of dawn, I could see the cuts on his face caked with blood. I winced. “I got an idea, Joe. I think I can get you outa here with a drag. You know, a travois.”

“You can carry me.” With his good hand, he grabbed the cup and sipped the broth, spilling most of it, but he chewed some of the meat floating in it. “Fireman carry. You can do it,” he said.

I shook my head. “Look where you’re hurt.” I patted my chest. “You’d be bouncing along with your wound on my shoulder. Trust me, Joe.”

I went to work with his Kabar and the rope I used to roll the moose. A travois is no tricky thing to build. It’s just a couple of long poles with some sticks tied across. I could put Joe on the litter and pick up one end and drag the other end along the ground. This was something Joe hadn’t taught me. I learned it by reading books when I was a daydreaming kid. Now it was real.

I worked at a steady pace, lifting, chopping, and tying until I had a rough drag constructed of two slender spruces trees tied together with smaller pieces crossing like ladder rungs. No big deal, but it seemed to take me a long time.

“Okay, Joe,” I said. “Hold on, brother.”

I padded the travois with one half of the moose hide and tied Joe tightly in the other so he was secure in a large, hairy cocoon. Then I rolled him onto the drag and strapped him with the last of the parachute cord. Joe was pale and silent. I was scared and tired. I helped get his arms free.

“Let’s go then,” I said. “Joe, you ready? You might have to hold on some.” No answer. No movement. Just a nod. We left the kill site with a bit of sun peeking through the trees and lighting Joe’s moose hanging under the green boughs of spruce. For the first time, I realized I wouldn't be shooting a moose this year and may never again have the chance.

I was wearing Joe's frame pack and found I could slip the ends of the poles into the straps of the pack so I was carrying with my shoulders and not just my hands. The load was heavy and cumbersome, especially on the uneven, soft ground. I only made it about twenty yards before I realized that I needed a path to follow if I was going to get anywhere. I thought Joe was unconscious, but I had my hands full navigating the travois through the woods.

"Hold on, Joe. I've gotta clear us a path." I knew the direction of the trail, so I left him and started walking that way looking for routes without fallen trees or hummocks. I walked about a hundred yards moving sticks and breaking branches that might trip me or snag the travois. Then I went back to Joe. It was slow going, and I was soaked in sweat. The weight made the straps cut into my shoulders, and every mossy hummock and berry bush seemed to grab at the travois like the forest itself was trying to keep us there.

I progressed about a hundred yards at a time, first walking ahead and clearing a path, then going back for Joe. We traveled about thirty minutes before I stopped to rest and Joe spoke for the first time in a while.

"You're beating the shit outa me," he said.

"I'm sorry. I'm trying to be careful. Christ, I thought you had passed out." I opened the canteen and took a swig, then offered the last of it to him.

Joe sipped the water. "First you shoot me, and now you're dragging me around like a dog with a dead rabbit. Is that any way to treat a brother?" He looked at my pained face as I made to apologize again. "I'm just shitting ya," he said. "You know that, right?"

"I know, I shit and fell in it," I said, trying to shake off the tight grip of my guilt with a little bravado. "But you had it coming. I'm just looking for a cliff to throw you off."

Joe laughed even though it made him groan from the pain. "I've been in worse."

I knew he was telling the truth, but that gave me no comfort. I stared across the open bog to the hill where trail waited, the trail that would lead to the truck, the truck stuck in a mudhole.

I took a deep breath and looked down at my brother. His face was swelling and scary. I said, "Shit, I'm sorry, Joe. I put us in jam, didn't I?"

"At least no one's chucking mortars at us," Joe said. "And it's not so damn hot you can't breathe. I don't ever want you to see what I've seen, Sam. They call it 'in the shit' for a reason."

I just nodded and stared at the trees. How could I answer that? What could I say then that wouldn't sound like a dumbass comment from somebody who didn't know enough to say anything? I felt like I was in the shit now, but that's because I didn't know any better. "No, Joe, I guess this ain't so bad." I picked up the ends of the travois. "Let's get this show on the road."

The warmth of the sun was passing through the patchy trees when we reached the base of the hill. At the top was the old trail we'd been driving on where we camped. The travois would drag easier on that trail. Once we got to the trail, it was just a mile to the truck.

The hill was as bad as I imagined it would be, and I climbed it with anger. My strength was gone. My energy was gone. All I had left was anger. Anger at my recklessness, anger at the goddamned muskeg, anger at the hill and all the work that still waited at the top of the hill.

I took the first two steps, then my foot slipped and I was on my face. I rose and took two more steps and had to move a rotten birch trunk. I swore and fell, rose and stepped. The travois's weight had somehow doubled. The straps burned my shoulders. Salty sweat burned my eyes and blurred my vision. Joe groaned a lot, and I kept looking back at him with his head flopping side to side as I lurched forward. I grabbed bushes to pull myself along that then broke or uprooted. I slipped back onto my belly and didn't want to get up. Each time anger fueled me to start again—to lift and pull and drag.

I couldn't let myself think of Joe and his wounds. There was only this hill to climb now. This damn hill, and then the trail would be there. Halfway up I stood with my hands on my hips and pumped air into my lungs, but the travois tried to pull me back down, so I moved on without rest. Each step seemed the last possible thing I had the strength to do, and each fall made me want to stay down. But I rose and I stepped once, then again and again. Swear, rise, step, fall. That's how I climbed that hill.

And then it was done. I poked my head through the brush into the open air and saw the trail. The flat, straight, lovely trail.

"Damn it, Joe! We're going to do it!"

I could hear Joe panting as hard as I was. "Christ! That ride up the hill was worse than getting shot."

I laughed. I felt bad about it, but I laughed. I finally felt like Joe might not die after all. "We need to get you to the truck and get warmed up." My voice was clear and unshaken like I knew what I was doing. Joe grunted, then we both lay there looking at the sky. Breathing.

Just as the hill was worse than I expected, the trail was better than I hoped. It was a grassy six-foot swath through the forest cut by some seismic oil exploration outfit. No logs to climb over, no tussocks, and only a couple of mudholes. And then I saw the truck and the tent and remains of the campfire.

Our camp and the truck to take us home were waiting across fifty yards of mud and water that I had forgotten about. "You're going to get wet," I said. Without waiting for an answer, I started across, letting the mud suck against my boots and splash up my legs. I kept my eyes on the truck and trudged through that last mess with only the fumes left in the tank of whatever fuel was I was going on. I stopped by the cold campfire and lowered the travois to the ground for the last time.

"You know, I think I'd rather walk on two broken legs than do that again," said Joe.

"Oh, now you tell me," I said. "That would have been easier for me too." I untied the ropes that strapped him on his litter and dragged two air mattresses and a sleeping bag over to him. I helped him out of the wet hide, onto the air mattress, and into the bag. I collected wood and brought it to the fire circle and soon had a cheery campfire. We watched the flames and drank water.

"Come on, Humpy," whispered Joe. "Get that coffee going."

"Oh, I was going to get the moose meat first," I said, not meaning it. I could barely stay on my feet. I was held up by force of habit. I turned out my duffel and found a clean T-shirt and sweatshirt. The dry clothes felt good against my skin and made me want dry pants and socks, but there was no time for that.

"That might have to wait. Don't you think? You're in no shape to haul a moose quarter across a muskeg. And I sure as hell can't help," Joe said.

"No shit, Sherlock. You're no help at all. Besides, I figure we probably ought to get you to a doctor." Strangely, I was lighter than I'd been in months, and suddenly I could breathe. "I guess you wanna fire me as a hunting partner," I said.

"Naw," said Joe. "You can't fire family." That statement hung in the air like a smoke ring, and we both stared at it. I tried to imagine what Joe was seeing.

I leaned over and tugged at the bloody bandage, then checked the splint on his leg. Joe pushed my hands away each time. "Let it be," he said. "Let it be."

I found a whiskey bottle under the truck seat with a couple of ounces left in it. That was the only painkiller we had, but Joe was glad to get it. I let him savor the burn of whiskey on his tongue and turned my eye to the mudhole with the truck in it. Water had collected around the tires and the rear bumper rested on the mud. I chuckled. "You know, Joe, I guess this is when I say we're not out of the woods yet."

Joe smiled. "Guess we could have dug that out yesterday instead of sitting around on our asses, but you know what Dad would say: 'Hindsight's better than foresight by a damn sight.'"

"Ain't that the truth." I leaned on the truck fender and studied the trees along the trail, wishing for a shovel.

"Get that Handyman jack and tie a rope to a tree, then the rope to the jack, and the jack to the truck. It'll pull that bitch outa there easy," said Joe.

"But first I have to jack up the rear end and put wood under the wheels so the bumper doesn't drag," I said. "And for that, I need something to eat." I slapped the hood of the truck.

I got out the last can of stew, opened it, and set it by the fire. "You watch this stew and keep the fire going while I cut some sticks to go under the tires. We'll have something to eat, then we can tackle this mess with a full stomach and a better attitude. And we've got some coffee left in the thermos."

Joe hadn't heard a word. At first it scared me, but then I realized he was asleep. I sat beside him and picked up the can of stew, eating it cold and washing it down with coffee straight from the thermos. I was lost for a time—I don't know how long. I just sat not thinking or doing anything beyond the canned stew and the coffee and feeding the fire.

"You look pretty deep in thought there. Thinking about that girl back at the pizza parlor?" I jumped when Joe said it and could only laugh.

"Just staring. Too tired to think." I handed him a spoon and the can of stew. "You slept awhile." His eyes were bright and alert, but the rest of his face was too much of a mess to communicate much, except his mouth. It was smiling.

"Yeah. Sleeping makes me hungry."

"Coffee's only pee warm," I said, holding out the thermos.

"Pee warm's better 'n ice cold, like my ass. The fire feels good though, Humpy. Who taught you that?"

"Somebody I knew once. He taught me good." This talk was warmer than the campfire that created a bow of lights over our heads and sending sparks into the sky.

"This is kinda fun, huh?" said Joe. "Any excuse for a campout, I say."

"Pretty nice. Except for the shootin' and bleedin' and draggin' part."

"Remember before 'Nam, I'd go campin' every chance I got. After I got home, I thought I'd never go again. But here we are, little brother!" Lying here by the truck, Joe was feeling safe. I was too.

I rearranged the coals on the fire and pulled up the hood on the sweatshirt under my hunting coat. "I remember once camping with you in that fancy Mustang. You took that coupe down onto the Matanuska River bottom and got it high centered. It took us all weekend to get it out of there."

"Damn, that was stupid." He gestured toward the truck. "I thought this scene looked familiar."

I looked at him closely. "You're feeling lots better, aren't you?"

"Yeah, not moving is making a big difference. Still hurts, but not make-you-sick hurt. I'm weak as hell though. Wish we'd brought some backstrap o' that moose with us."

"Yeah, I should have. When we get home though we'll eat the whole thing, breaded and fried little steaks with Mom's gravy."

"Yeah," said Joe. "That might be the best eatin' of the moose."

Joe fell asleep again. I wanted to start getting the truck out of the mud but I didn't want to wake him, so I dozed a bit then changed into dry socks. I thought about facing Mom and explaining what happened. I wished I had Iris to talk me through it, but she wasn't here and maybe wouldn't be there for me back home.

When Joe woke up, I said, "Mom's going to kill me, you know."

"Naw. She'll blame me and read me the riot act. I can hear it now. *What in the hell were you thinking? The two of you act like you don't have a brain between you.*"

I thought that was pretty accurate, but thinking about facing Mom shook me up, so I changed the subject. "So, you know you asked me about the girl at Polar Pizza?"

"Yeah. What about her?"

I picked up the stew can and scraped the last of it onto my spoon. I wished I had more. "Well, I was really into her until I found out she was married. You could have fooled me the way she acted. I tell you, Joe, she didn't act married most of the time."

Joe fussed around trying to light a cigarette, then gave up and leaned back to rest. "I told you she had her eye on you. So did you do anything about it? She could probably teach you a thing or two. Older woman and all."

"It wasn't like that." I tried to figure out what it was like with Julie, and then with Iris. "I'm kinda chasing another girl."

"I think I saw her with you. Cute little brunette flower child? Kinda flat chested, but some potential. You getting anywhere?"

"Not really. I mean, I was . . . for a while, but I think she just wants to be friends now, if even that."

"There you go."

"What do you mean?"

Joe laughed and shook the last cigarette out of the pack and lit it. "She opened the door, man. She's saying, 'Hang out and be close to me so I can see if I like you.'" He reached a hand out to the fire.

"She didn't like it when I got in that fight. She thinks I'm a little too wild. Fancy that."

"Hang in there with her. You'll bring her around."

I got to my feet and stood looking at the truck in the mudhole and thinking that's how I was with Iris. I was mired, couldn't move in either direction. Maybe we had to be *just buds* like she said at the beginning, but that wasn't going to be easy. "I don't know, Joe. I just don't understand women. I can't seem to figure them out."

Joe turned his head to look at me. "You know, one of your hippie gurus would say that this is the first step to enlightenment."

"What is?"

"Knowing what you don't know," said Joe.

I climbed into the bed of the truck and tossed out the Handyman jack and a coil of rope, then hopped down and walked back to the fire. When I pushed my hand in my coat pocket, I found a Snickers candy bar. I broke it and tossed half across the fire to my brother.

Acknowledgments

First a deep bow my editor, Michelle McCann, whose frank conversations and honest critique helped build a strong story. Thanks to Olivia Ngai's eye for detail and strong support for the story I was trying to tell, which helped the book and the writer grow. My reader friends Nancy Fisher and Patty See surrounded me with support and the readers' love of language and story. My wife, Madelyn, was always there with a hand on my back when I wavered, a critical ear tuned to the writer's voice, and the patience needed to live with a writer.

Dan L. Walker grew up in Alaska with a brother who fought in the Vietnam War and returned home with PTSD. Dan is a high school teacher as well as an author, and has published blogs, essays, articles, and fiction in magazines and literary journals, including *Alaska Magazine* and the *Journal of Geography.* His first book on Sam Barger, *Secondhand Summer,* represented the state of Alaska at the Library of Congress National Book Festival in 2017 and was on Alaska's Battle of the Books list. Visit DanLWalker.com for more.

CPSIA information can be obtained
at www.ICGtesting.com
Printed in the USA
BVHW042155180221
600432BV00006B/19